IF THE FATES ALLOW

CHLOE I. MILLER

KEY LIME BOOKS

Book Cover by Books and Moods

Editor: Samantha Swart

Proofreader: Jan Hurst

Haven House Art: Wisp (IG: wisp_tale)

Kindle E-Book ASIN: B0CP7FGYX7

Paperback ISBN: 979-8-9876201-8-2

For Dr. Merissa Hudson

Thank you for being my found family, especially during the holidays.
I can't wait to go out Golden Girls' style with you.

Contents

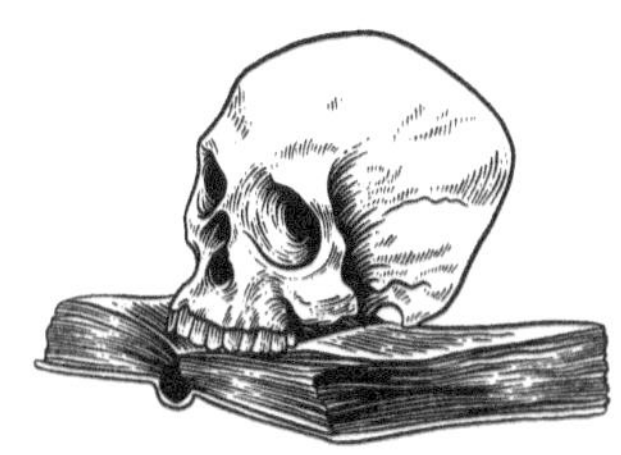

CONTENT WARNINGS

If The Fates Allow features elements of manipulation, abuse, **strong** sexual content, profanity, and various forms of murder.

There is also a brief mentioning of pigs, a lengthy discussion on goats, and a horse who might secretly be a feminist.

Music plays a large role in the Haven House series, and to receive the most immersive experience possible, we invite you to explore the novel's soundtrack.

www.chloeimiller.com/playlists

If The Fates Allow

SOUNDTRACK

Dearest Reader,

If this is your first time entering the world of Haven House, please allow me to welcome you with open arms and... provide you with a warning. This novella is dark, with twists and turns waiting around every corner. The idea was to craft a deliciously gothic tale for the holiday season, and I think we've accomplished that with this story featuring the very last of the Fairweathers to ever reside at Haven House.

But who are the Fairweathers, you ask? Well, that requires a terribly long answer, so I'll say the Fairweathers are a family who came to the Florida panhandle in the latter half of the eighteenth century, ready and willing to seek their fortune in the area's blossoming lumber business. The land they settled on was not but a mile from the powder white sands of the Gulf Coast and was truly an ideal spot for a mill with its various bayous winding through the surrounding marshlands.

From there, an empire was born.

Wait. No. It wasn't exactly an empire. Not yet, at least. It will take generations of Fairweathers before the word empire ever crosses anyone's lips. The books in the Haven House series show us the Fairweathers of today, but this novella gives us the middle of their story and provides a glimpse of the family during a time when their business sits on the brink of great success.

And Fairweathers will do *anything* to achieve success.

I hope you enjoy Willa's novella. If you're a regular reader of the series, hints of this famous Fairweather's story have been sprinkled throughout the books. The sick feeling that chases Liam while he explores the forest trails in *The Secrets That You Keep,* the dread that seizes Evie as she's led to the graveyard in *Our Lips Are Sealed,* and finally, the chorus of voices mixing with those of Jamison's long lost loved ones in *Somebody's Watching Me.*

The origin of it all is here. This novella is meant to be a fun read, but it will also remind you that in the world of Haven House, perspective is everything and that our villains rarely know they're villains until it's too late.

Happy Reading,
Chloe

CHAPTER I

1887

R^{*ain.*}

Wilhelmina Fairweather loved the rain.

She loved the thunder and the lightning, the way the sky melted from its usual colorful hues to a miserable gray, and how it washed away the stench of her father's mill, forcing everyone indoors to live life as she did.

For as long as she could remember, rain always arrived whenever the clock struck three. Morning or night. In the summer, in the spring, or even now, during the autumnal march of the fall season, one could set a watch to the prompt torrential downpours that fell upon Haven House in the three o'clock hours.

And even though she might love the rain, it did not love her in return. The damp, sticky air never sat well in her lungs, and while beautiful to witness on days like today, it was yet another thing that kept her trapped inside.

Ignoring the book in her lap, Willa gazed up at the splatter of water beating down on the glass panes of the conservatory's ceiling. The fall harvest would begin in a few days, and her afternoons of enjoying the roar of Mother Nature's daily temper tantrums would end once winter approached.

Which was fine, in Willa's opinion. Cooler weather meant more time outdoors and, most importantly, more freedom away from her family.

Thunder rumbled close enough to rattle the oil lamp on the table next to her lounger, and she reached over to twist the knob for a brighter flame. With the darkening clouds overhead, she didn't want to waste another second of this perfectly cozy afternoon. The entire day was shaping up quite nicely between the dreary atmosphere and the deliciously gothic story in her book. If things continued as they were, she could read until nightfall, snuggled under a blanket, with no one else around to bother her.

"Your mother is looking for you."

Or perhaps not.

Setting the book aside, Willa shifted to address her mother's companion standing in the doorway on the conservatory's upper level. The staff at Haven House understood to keep their distance, allowing her to have this slice of heaven to herself.

"Tell her I'm coming, Bonnie."

Bonnie was the only exception to the unspoken no-entry rule, and as she crossed the room's threshold, the woman's pert nose wrinkled at the chaos the space held. Riddled with stacks of books and various papers holding stories jotted down when the mood struck, the conservatory would appear out of sorts to most people. Yet for Willa, the books and foolish scribbles of her mind equated to a land of daydreams and lives lived far beyond Haven House.

Her imagination ran free in the conservatory, making this long, boring life bearable.

"It's raining," Bonnie observed. "You know I don't like it when you sit down there during a storm. The dampness clings to the air on the lower level."

"I'm fine, Bonnie."

Sickly since childhood, Willa suffered bouts of lung spasms, which hindered her ability to breathe properly. She could never keep the company of crowds for too long or enjoy the outdoors throughout the year like her siblings did. The conservatory functioned as a personal sanctuary, built exclusively for her use during one of the worst bouts of illness ever to strike. Those arduously painful months just so happened to coincide with a massive renovation under her mother's direction, and, wanting to give her daughter some semblance of normalcy, Margaret Fairweather convinced her husband to build Willa a place that would allow her to experience the world without actually living in it.

"Always so stubborn," Bonnie grumbled, snapping her fingers. At the popping sound, felines of every shape and color emerged from their hiding places, ready to follow their pied piper. "It's the Fairweather in you."

Her message delivered, Bonnie left with a parade of cats behind her, slipping off into the main hall where Haven's staff rushed about in preparation for her brother's arrival home. Wanting to have nothing to do with it, Willa's shoulders slumped, and she groaned over being summoned. Cal had been away earning a college education this past year, which was a total waste of time, in her opinion. A college degree didn't matter. Not when you were the sole male heir of the Fairweather family. The mill was Cal's future, and there was no way to change that.

Swinging her feet to the ground, Willa stood with an annoyed huff. She took one last look at the watery view, extinguished the lamp, and placed her book on the nearest bookshelf. Undoubtedly, she wouldn't be able to return to finish the novel today. If her mother wanted an audience, it wasn't without good reason. As of late, Margaret Fairweather didn't care to spend time with her offspring, finding them as dull as she did Haven House.

Taking the small set of steps to the upper level, she entered the hall and weaved through the bustling traffic of people. While searching for her mother, Willa waved a hand in front of her face, feeling a bit like an idiot as she did. On her last visit to Mr. Abernathy, he claimed that the flapping of one's hand in front of the face was an effective method in warding off potential illnesses, and her mother had insisted she follow his instructions.

Personally, Willa thought the idea was a load of horse shit.

More than likely, her mother did as well, only forcing the ridiculous behavior on Willa to satisfy her never-ending desire for control. Alone in this vast wasteland of pine, without any hint of gentry or society for miles, no one was exempt from being used as entertainment for Margaret Fairweather.

Knowing she would probably find her mother in the newly expanded ballroom, Willa headed there first. With the upcoming fall harvest came the annual Fairweather Gathering, a hosted event for a handful of affluent Hollingsdale families—all two of them—and other fellow lumber barons within a close radius of the Fairweather Mill. Partners at the best of times, enemies at the worst, her father's associates were a mixed lot of like-minded men who were as pleasant to be around as an agitated beehive.

As predicted, she found her mother in the ballroom, fussing at the staff while they decorated. Willa smartly waited in the doorway until noticed and catching sight of her, Margaret heaved out a sigh. "Wilhelmina, will you please straighten your spine. That posture of yours is atrocious."

Out of reflex, Willa did as she was told. Her mother ruled with an iron fist, and disobedience was something that only occurred in other households.

"Did you need me?"

"Lucinda's dress." Margaret swept a hand in the direction of her youngest child standing in the ballroom's corner. "Do you have an opinion on it?"

Willa wanted to say she had a great number of opinions on a great number of things, but dresses were not one of them. "I like it," she replied. "What do you think, Lucy?"

Poor Lucy looked miserable, staring out the windows with her shoulders slouched. "It's acceptable," she mumbled, obviously displeased by the choice. "If I cannot wear my lovely blue dress, I suppose this brown one will do."

"Yes," their mother agreed. "It *will* do."

Smoothing a hand down the skirt, Lucy's lips twisted in disgust. "It matches my eyes, at least."

"It matches your hair, too," Willa offered. "Almost perfectly, I would say."

Tears welled in her sister's eyes, and Willa winced. At seventeen, Lucy never missed an opportunity to be dramatic. "I do not have brown hair!" she screeched, patting the bun on her head, which was made up of the brownest hair ever to exist. "My hair is auburn. Why do you have to be so terrible to me, Willa?"

The corners of their mother's mouth curved upward, the growing smile a signal of her displeasure. Lucy was well past the age of having childish fits, and this outburst would only fuel Margaret's spite.

"Lucinda, if you cannot behave, you will not attend The Gathering." Margaret clasped her hands in front of her, circling the room at a measured pace. "I hear Violet Templeton will be in attendance. Perhaps she can entertain Paul Anderson since you won't be able to join us."

Paul Anderson was one of the county's most eligible bachelors and the only son of Ulrich Anderson, owner of a massive sawmill just down the bayou from Haven House. There were whispers that he and a couple of his cousins were arriving today with Cal, the four of them traveling down from the north together.

Poor Lucy had loved Paul from the moment she laid eyes on him, and last year, they heard from Cal that their father had made an agreement with Ulrich Anderson regarding the pair.

"I was only joking." The tears in Lucy's eyes quickly evaporated. Their mother could not abide crying in any form, and even if Lucy were prepared to weather her wrath, she would never give up the chance to spend time with Paul. "I know my hair is mousy brown."

Margaret halted in the center of the room. "I wouldn't go that far, but it is most assuredly not a beautiful chestnut like Willa's."

Their mother excelled at pitting them against one another. It was a new phase—one none of them cared for—but thankfully, Willa and her siblings caught on before any damage could be truly done.

Lucy's cheeks turned a light shade of pink. "No one has hair as beautiful as Willa's."

If they had been alone, Willa would have snorted at her sister's poor acting. Lucy was the beauty between the two of them. At three and twenty, Willa was well past her prime and readily preparing for an inevitable life of spinsterhood.

Or, in other words, *heaven*.

Because what woman wouldn't want a life consisting not of marital duties but of napping and books?

"Thank you, Lucy," Willa replied, knowing she had to lay it on thick so their mother would believe the charade. She and Lucy would laugh about this later, as they usually did. "One day, you might achieve a shade as lovely as mine, but for now, I'm afraid you'll just have to deal with that horse's mane of yours."

Lucy's eyes narrowed in outrage. "Horse's mane?"

Perhaps the insult went too far, but there was no going back. "Well, what color would you relate it to?" Willa examined her nails as if bored. "I thought we all just agreed that you're not exactly mousey. Naturally, a step up would be a horse."

Sucking in a deep breath, Lucy fisted her hands at her side. "Mother, do you need me for anything else?"

Their mother's smile widened. "No, you are dismissed."

Careful not to stomp out of the room, Lucy held her head high as she exited.

"I expect you to behave during The Gathering, Wilhelmina," her mother warned once Lucy was gone. "I've invited John Richards, and he has sent word that he will be joining us."

Oh, no.

Her days of spinsterhood flashed before her eyes, destined to be lost forever thanks to the circulating rumor that Willa was headed towards a life of marital *bliss*. Ten years her senior and on a wifely hunt, John Richards was on the lookout for someone to care not only for himself but also for his six offspring. The gossip on their last visit to Hollingsdale said that Mr. Richards had narrowed his choices to three women, with Willa being one of them.

Her father had been thrilled with the idea. Mr. Richards possessed a large farm on the outskirts of town. Good land, according to her father. The kind of land he could use to increase Fairweather's pine production.

"You'll want to make an impression," her mother continued. "Wear Lucy's blue dress."

Wear the dress your sister wanted to wear is what she meant. Lucy would understand, but it didn't make the betrayal hurt any less for Willa. "Yes, mother."

The sound of hurried footsteps and a murmur of excitement carried about in the hall, and Margaret's stern expression melted immediately into rapt anticipation. "That would be your brother," she said, rushing from the room to greet her favorite child. "He mentioned something about traveling with friends in his letter. Do not antagonize them like you did the last ones who visited."

All of Calvin's friends were arrogant rotters. They were often the eldest sons of wealthy families, doing nothing with their lives, and how her brother convinced them to come home with him was beyond Willa's understanding. Of course, thanks to her mother's wildly expensive expansion, their home sat in grand splendor compared to the other estates in the area.

However, to Willa, Haven House would always be just a boring little corner of the world where nothing exciting happened, and only the Fairweathers ever stayed for very long.

"You know it's just the Andersons," Willa said to her mother's departing figure. "No one important."

And while it might be only Paul and his cousins stopping in on their way to the Anderson estate, Willa decided to join in on the homecoming.

Cal would one day control her future if she were lucky enough to remain a spinster, and she needed to keep in his good graces.

Not that she didn't like her brother. Cal was smart and would do well in control of the Fairweather lumber business. He had their father's brains. The two men were almost identical in the way they reasoned over things with the main difference being that Cal didn't hold the same heavy-handed strictness as their father. Cold and calculating, Stephen Fairweather thankfully never bothered with his children, saving his ferocious temper for his workers and his wife. During the times their mother fell victim to his violent outbursts, even the high-handed Margaret would smartly go silent.

Coming out of the ballroom, Willa made her way to the front of the house and found her mother holding Cal in a tight embrace as if she were afraid he would leave again.

"My beautiful boy," Margaret cooed, cradling the back of his head. "As handsome as ever."

A handsome face was something else Cal had that their father didn't. With his light hair and smooth complexion, Cal took after their mother's side of the family.

Willa wasn't so lucky. One of the worst insults of her life had been when Great Aunt Regalia had come for a visit and announced—quite loudly—upon meeting Willa that she carried the look of the Fairweathers through and through.

She hadn't wanted to admit the old bat was right, but Willa couldn't deny her dark, deep-set eyes, much too high cheekbones, and upturned nose. Every inch of her face was a testament to her Fairweather lineage, and as unfortunate as that was, she truly didn't mean to look so very vexed all the time.

It just came naturally.

"Hey!" Catching her on approach, Cal hugged her with one arm, grinning like the prodigal son that he was. "How are you, Willa?"

Her mother hated the nickname but never spoke against her brother using it. "Don't crowd her, Cal." Margaret pushed at Willa's shoulders, trying to worm her way back into the embrace. "We don't need her going into one of her fits."

With an eye roll, Willa stepped aside and collided with a man waiting for the reunion between mother and son to lose steam. He had a friendly smile, and she didn't bother to wait for her brother to make formal introductions.

"You must be one of Paul's cousins?" She stuck out her hand. "I'm Wilhelmina Fairweather. Welcome to Haven House."

He grinned at her forwardness. "Beau Anderson."

They shook hands, and Willa noted how much the man looked like Paul. "Are you really here to help with the Anderson's mill during the fall and winter seasons?"

"That I am, but not just for the fall and winter." His smile widened. "When Paul takes over Anderson Lumber, I'll come on to function as his secondary."

"And where is Paul?" Willa asked, peeking around the man to see if Lucy's true love was anywhere around. "Is he here?"

"Paul went ahead to the house. He was anxious to see his mother."

Beau seemed so much nicer than the other Andersons. They were a close family but held a sharp edge to them at times. "I hear Paul is graduating in the spring. Will you be doing the same?"

"No, I've graduated already, and will stay on to learn what I can while Paul finishes school," Beau replied. "However, Noah can only tend to the workers until the new year before heading north. He has job prospects waiting, unless my aunt can persuade him to stay on, too."

"Noah?"

"My older brother." Beau inclined his head to the doorway behind her. "He spotted your library, and I'm afraid we've lost him to it. Noah can't pass up a good book."

Second to the conservatory, the library was Willa's favorite room at Haven House. "What do you mean, he'll be tending to the workers?"

"Noah is a doctor," Beau explained, pride evident in his voice. "Studied under Osler and everything."

She had no idea what that meant, but it sounded important. "Well, you are both welcome at Haven House."

"I thought Noah could take a look at you, Willa," Cal said, finally breaking free from their mother. "He's a right genius and maybe can help you."

Anything had to be better than Mr. Abernathy. Other than telling her to flap a hand or to try praying her affliction away, the man wasn't much help. She was only required to see him because he was cheap.

But now, in the presence of a proper doctor, a twinge of giddiness struck Willa, and she excitedly hurried across the foyer to the library.

"Where are you going?" Margaret hissed, appalled over her abrupt departure while a guest was present. "Cease your running this instant."

"I'm sorry." Willa waved a hand over her shoulder. "But if this Noah Anderson is to be my doctor, I suppose I should introduce myself."

CHAPTER 2

Willa was wrong.

She should have stayed in the foyer.

Or, at the very least, she should have entered the library quietly instead of exploding into the room like a stampeding elephant.

When she came in, Dr. Anderson's back was to her, and only his broad shoulders and height registered at first. He was enormous and browsing the floor-to-ceiling bookshelves, which suddenly looked much smaller with him in front of them.

"Dr. Anderson?"

Speaking his name caused her new savior to turn around, and once he did, Willa was struck mute.

Silenced by a handsome face.

And not merely handsome. No, that word was simply too lackluster to describe the man before her. Standing there with her eyes wide, and mouth gaping open, she decided that calling him handsome showed a complete lack of imagination, and, if there was one thing for certain, Wilhelmina Fairweather had imagination in spades.

Yet, at this very moment, it was failing her.

A poet was needed. Yes, that was it. A grand master of the craft who could properly express how the good doctor's crystal blue eyes and luscious full lips melded so seamlessly with his chiseled features and tan skin. And how his midnight black hair and shadow of a beard only added to the allure.

She was well aware she was rudely staring, having never glimpsed such a man in all her life, but she could not stop herself. It was as if an exotic fairy tale creature had fled the pages of her books and come to visit Haven House, daring to beguile them with its beauty.

And then he went and did the most horrendous thing possible, catapulting the situation from mildly uncomfortable to dire in under a second.

Dr. Noah Anderson smiled.

Good heavens.

Could a heart stop from witnessing a mere presentation of teeth? Willa certainly never thought it possible, but here she was, lightheaded and unable to focus.

"Wilhelmina Fairweather?"

Her eyes went even wider. The way he said her name had goosebumps breaking out across her skin. She could almost taste the rich timbre in his voice, and it reminded her of the time she drank a glass of her father's whiskey on a cold winter's night. The amber liquid had slid down her throat with a heated caress, warming her insides as it made its way to her belly.

A dark eyebrow arched when she remained silent. "You are Ms. Wilhelmina Fairweather, are you not?"

The friendly tone there a moment ago now held a hint of annoyance, sparking her own temper. How dare he come here with a face like that and presume she could carry on a civil conversation.

"Ms. Fairweather," he drawled, propping one of his muscled shoulders on a bookcase. "Are you alright?"

She nodded, although perhaps a little too enthusiastically. "Yes."

A lie, of course, but there was no other choice. It was the best she could do without looking like a complete fool, and for him to expect her to articulate any piece of information about herself since he turned around was a ludicrous assumption on his part.

"Are you sure?"

"I'm fine." The farthest thing from fine, Willa fanned herself, attempting to cool the growing rush of heat that bordered on the obscene. "Thank you for inquiring."

"So, you are Wilhelmina?"

He straightened to step closer, and she instinctively retreated until her back met the wall, knocking a framed picture askew.

"Ye-yes," she croaked, wondering how he could have such a well-defined jawline. Surely, having such a feature and flaunting it so brazenly must be illegal. "I am Wilhelmina Fairweather."

Understanding something was off, he halted in his advance. That perfect jawline ticking as he surveyed her state. "I'm Paul Anderson's cousin."

"The doctor," she replied nervously. "You are the doctor, and I am Wilhelmina."

"Cal asked that I examine you. He mentioned your lung issues, and I can already see I have my work cut out for me."

Pressing her lips together, she attempted to quell her rapid breathing, not wanting him to realize what was currently happening had nothing to do with lung spasms.

"Nod, if you understand, Ms. Fairweather."

Dear God, did he think her a simpleton? She couldn't fault him for it, but still, he could have the decency not to make a show of it.

Willa stuck her nose in the air. "I quite understand."

"Good." He returned to the bookshelves and continued searching through the selections. "By the way, your Keats collection is lacking."

"Only because I do not care for Keats."

"Well, there's no accounting for taste." Sliding a novel from its spot, he flipped through the pages. "However, I see you have two copies of *The*

Modern Prometheus. I know Cal's not a reader, so I assume this is either yours or one of your sisters, and I find that interesting."

"Why is that interesting?"

His big shoulders shrugged. "Even though it was written by a woman, most of the females in my life can't handle it. They find the story disturbing."

It was her turn to arch an eyebrow. "Perhaps it's time you associate with women who have stronger stomachs."

And there was his taunting smile again.

"May I borrow it?" Snapping the book closed, he held it in the air. "Reading of Dr. Frankenstein and his monster always seems fitting this time of year when we lose the heat of summer and trade it for dreary autumn skies."

"You may," she replied. "And I happen to enjoy autumn. Summer and spring are my least favorite seasons."

"Why is that?"

If he were truly planning to treat her ailments, she shouldn't keep things from him, but with honesty came a price. A lesson learned from her mother. Being open and honest with another person provided them with ammunition to use against you later.

"My spasms lessen once the heat departs," she explained. "I can spend time outdoors if I choose to."

Her description intrigued him. "You said spasms. Is that what it feels like?"

Moving off her spot on the wall, she nodded. "I cough and cough but can never get it under control. Then I lose my breath. It feels as if I'm empty of oxygen and can't replace it fast enough."

Hearing her symptoms had him crossing the room. Without permission, he laid a hand on the flat of her back and another on her lower rib cage. "Breathe in and out for me."

A blush seeped into her cheeks, but she did as he asked, focusing on the opposite wall. "I'll bring my bag on the next visit," he murmured, closing his eyes to focus while she inhaled and exhaled. "We need to gather a baseline before I recommend treatment."

Dr. Noah Anderson smelled as lovely as he looked, and his scent overpowered her with every draw of air through her nostrils. Sighing, she took a moment to enjoy his nearness.

"Why don't you like Keats?"

Eyes still closed, he had whispered the question, and Willa prayed for her heart to remain at its current pace. "I much prefer Poe if I am to read poetry, and I also enjoy his shorter narratives."

The hand on her rib cage slid higher, his thumb grazing the underside of a breast. The touch had been unintentional, but even so, it didn't halt the flood of salacious thoughts from taking over Willa's brain.

Once last year, while on one of her winter walks through the forest, she happened upon a worker from the mill secretly meeting with his sweetheart. The couple had no inkling of her presence and kissed with such abandon that Willa had stopped, transfixed by the sight.

And she still didn't move as they carried on, not even when the mill worker opened the woman's shirt to lavish her breasts with his tongue. It had been wrong to watch, but a jealous curl of yearning had left Willa frozen, the pain reminding her that this brazen act of passion was something she would never have. It became even worse when, in a frenzy, the woman dropped to her knees and tried to lower the man's pants.

Willa had left the couple then, returning to Haven House with the bitterness of a pathetic destiny in her mouth. Fate would never allow her to know pleasure like she had witnessed out there in the forest. It would never give her a moment of feeling unrestricted and adored. Destiny had dictated early on that no man would ever desire her in the way the mill worker had desired his woman that day. She would forever live feeling like she was alone in the world, married or not.

"Murder and mayhem, is it?" Opening his eyes again, Noah grinned down at her. "From a person who owns multiple copies of *The Modern Prometheus*, I suppose I shouldn't be surprised."

Breathless from having him this close and with the irony of being in such a state not lost on her, Willa returned his smile. "I do love my monsters."

Neither said anything for a long minute, each studying the other carefully. Noah, likely doing so for scientific purposes, while her reasons fell more along the lines of committing every perfect line of his face to memory.

"Do you wish to tame them?" he asked softly. "The monsters, I mean."

"What's the good in loving a monster if you wish to tame it?" The corners of her mouth tilted upward, the movement drawing his gaze. "They're created to wreak havoc, and suppressing a monster's nature would be unfair. Let them run wild, I say."

"And have you ever run wild, Ms. Fairweather?"

Her mother chose that moment to sweep into the room. "Dr. Anderson, I am Margaret Fairweather, the Lady of Haven House."

Unbothered by her mother's glacial stare, Noah removed his hands. "It is lovely to meet you, Mrs. Fairweather. I was chatting with your daughter while admiring this lovely library."

Margaret didn't seem impressed, which wasn't a surprise to Willa. "According to my son, you might be able to help us deal with Wilhelmina?"

Deal with Wilhelmina.

Her father wasn't the only one excited by Willa's possible betrothal to John Richards and eventual departure from Haven House. Stephen and Margaret Fairweather never agreed on anything except for this. Grace, the firstborn, had been their favorite, and Cal would forever be the golden son. Lucy was the baby of the family, but it was different with Willa. They tolerated her but not much else.

Noah must have heard the undercurrent in her mother's statement and frowned. "I'll do my best to help your daughter in any way I can, Mrs. Fairweather."

"And what assessment have you come up with thus far?"

"Nothing as of yet," he replied, brows knitted together as he took the two of them in. "We were becoming acquainted over Keats and monsters made by men."

The heavy oak front door of Haven House slammed shut, rattling the walls of the library. The sound elicited a grimace from both Willa and her mother.

"While at Haven House, you'll do well to remember that men themselves can also be the monsters, Dr. Anderson," Margaret said as her husband's gruff commands echoed in from the foyer. "They don't always need to create them."

Stiff from standing silently in the parlor's corner, Willa stifled a yawn. Lucy caught her eye and, likely just as sore, did the same.

Two hours.

Every female in the room had stood at attention for two excruciating hours while Willa's father held court with Cal and the Anderson brothers. The talk ranged from her brother's adventures at school to the local lumber business before finally landing on Beau and Noah's *rank*, as her father called it, within the Anderson clan.

"As the eldest, I would think it should be you instead of Beau becoming Paul's second," her father stated, grilling Noah yet again on his choice of becoming something as ridiculous as a doctor. "Why waste your time? There's no money in medicine."

The flicker of annoyance Willa had witnessed earlier now shone deeply in Noah's eyes. Unlike every other living creature within a fifty-mile radius of Haven House, he wasn't afraid of her father and had sat politely, albeit irritated, through the barrage of questions.

"I don't find helping others to be a waste of time," Noah replied coolly from his spot on the settee next to his brother. "There are many who are unable to receive the care they might need due to a lack of people practicing proper medicine."

Not caring for the answer, Stephen Fairweather reclined in the wingback across from the Anderson brothers. Calvin sat a few feet from their father in the secondary wingback while Willa's mother stood behind him, suffering along with her daughters. Bonnie did the same, never leaving Margaret's side.

"Take Willa, for example." Noah gestured in her direction, and Willa felt herself blushing all over again. Not since they exited the library had he even spared her a glance. "From what I've learned, she would benefit from the aid of someone like me."

Her father's head rolled on his thick neck to give her a once over, and the heat brought on by Noah's attention quickly turned to ice. "Mr. Abernathy has kept her alive this long," he grumbled. "Willa's care and upkeep are not a poor man's endeavor."

Noah's strained, polite smile slid into a hard line, and Beau shifted uncomfortably beside him. "An endeavor I'm sure you, as a loving father, take on with the utmost reverence," Noah said. "There is no greater gift than having the means to care for a sick child."

Willa almost felt sorry for the poor Anderson brothers when her father's attention returned to them. "It's like an investment, you see. Willa is no beauty, but not as bad off as that homely Sanderson girl prancing around Hollingsdale society currently."

Noah's dark brows snapped together. "I'm afraid I don't understand."

Stephen Fairweather was never one to mince words, and while her family often foolishly hoped for the best when he opened his mouth, Willa quickly surmised that today would be no exception.

"Even at her advanced age, Willa has caught the eye of a newly made bachelor. A man who owns the largest plot of untapped fertile land in the area," her father explained. "If I can have it in exchange for Willa, well then, that will make up for the expense she has caused us and will one day provide a profit after I use the land to expand."

Observing her father's words sink into Noah and Beau's brains was a bit like watching a magnificent ship sinking spectacularly into the ocean. Willa was no expert on the matter but had read extensively on such things, mystified by the accounts of survivors. The slow, shocked expressions on the brothers' faces deepened the more her father's statement penetrated their minds and—metaphorically speaking, of course—reminded her of how she thought those poor ship passengers might have looked as they went down.

"Richards will be at The Gathering, correct?" Cal asked. "If he's serious about Willa, I'd like to speak with him. There's a section of land in Hollingsdale I've had my eye on. It's an ideal spot for us to build a second Fairweather homestead, and it turns out that John Richards holds the deed." Her brother aimed a grin at her. "Perhaps Willa can give him one of her sweet smiles, and we'll nab an extra piece of the pie while we're at it."

Both Anderson brothers paled while her mother looked positively aglow over the idea of moving to town. "Gentlemen, please remember that Mr. Richards' interest in Wilhelmina is merely speculation. We'll have to wait and see how he engages with her before any plans can be made."

Noah's eyes snapped to Willa, but she refused to look at him, keeping her gaze trained ahead, just as her father preferred.

"Are you saying you've had no interaction with this Richards person and are considering his hand in marriage?" Noah asked, sounding somewhat angry. When she didn't reply, he turned to Cal. "Is he aware of her illness?"

The question hurt, and unable to hold her tongue, Willa finally spoke. "I am more than my illness, Dr. Anderson. I will make a good wife to John Richards or any man lucky enough to have me."

Her father's harsh laughter filled the parlor. "You are an invalid who offers no value. Lucky would be the very last word I would use to describe the man willing to take you on, Wilhelmina."

Embarrassment singed her cheeks, but Willa showed no emotion at his jab, having been taught the consequences should she do so.

Beau cleared his throat. "Will there be many people at The Gathering tomorrow?" he asked, obviously searching for another topic. "My brother and I have already been informed we're attending."

"Oh, yes!" her mother said, seizing the opportunity. Margaret's heart might be black, but she despised her husband and would never give him the satisfaction of knowing how his comments hurt one of them. "We should have well over sixty guests."

"Oh, I would say we're closer to a hundred at my last count," Bonnie said proudly. "It will be a lovely Gathering this year."

Noah abruptly stood, moving around the center table where the tea service was arranged. "My apologies."

"Uh, yes." Beau joined him, looking rather relieved to be leaving. "We really must be going."

Willa allowed her gaze to roam, and like a moth to a flame, it connected directly with Noah's. She thought he must have no manners at all since he dared to openly stare at her from across the room. "My apologies," he repeated when he knew he held her attention. "I look forward to helping in any way I can."

"As long as you're not expecting us to pay, Dr. Anderson," her father said sarcastically. "Wilhelmina is yours to do with as you like."

CHAPTER 3

"**A** horse?"

Lucy brushed her hair furiously while seated at the vanity in her bedroom's corner. "You had to call me a horse?"

Willa chuckled as she watched a snowy egret traverse the bayou's waterline from Lucy's window. She could only spot the one white figure, but as sunset approached, more would arrive to have their dinner on the swampy shore.

"It was the best insult I could come up with," she replied. "You know I don't do well when put on the spot."

"And the blue dress." Lucy swiveled around on the stool. "She forces you to wear the blue dress when it looks much better on me."

Willa didn't care what she wore and would gladly strip out of the dress right then so as not to have to listen to her sister complain all night. "It doesn't matter what you wear, Lucy. You're beautiful, and Paul Anderson will trip over himself to have your attention."

"Mother would never have done that to Grace."

Long gone from Haven House, their mother remained dedicated to her eldest daughter. "No, she most definitely would not have done that to Grace."

With the afternoon sun disappearing, the temperature would be ideal for a stroll. Tentatively opening the balcony door, Willa let the first slap of cool air strike her lungs. Perfect.

"Come walk with me, Lucy."

Setting her brush aside, Lucy joined her, and the two of them stepped outside to walk along Haven's expansive balcony, which traveled the entire length of the second floor. Careful to keep out of sight so they wouldn't be seen by arriving guests, they headed towards the rear of the house arm and arm.

"Are you feeling good about The Gathering tonight?" Lucy asked.

Willa nodded, looking out over the dozens of oaks sprinkled across the lawn. Their home's beauty was unmatched during this time of day. Nestled in the thick pine forests of northern Florida and less than a mile from the powder white dunes of the Gulf of Mexico, the splendor of Haven House was hard to deny. "I'll remain on the stairs. Standing above all, as if I'm an angel on judgment day, ready to condemn the slightest hint of wickedness."

Lucy scoffed. "This party is being thrown by Mother. The only wickedness that could occur will be if Paul's mother drinks too much punch and tries to hire Bonnie out from under us yet again."

"That was quite the scandal last year."

"I don't know if Mother has ever forgiven her."

Stopping to lay a hip on the railing, Willa observed her sister. Brown dress or not, Lucy remained dazzling. "And what about you?" she asked. "Are you feeling good about tonight?"

"I've missed Paul." Lucy released a sigh so thick with longing it nearly sent Willa tumbling over the railing. "I can't tell you how hard it's been to restrain myself from marching right over there now that he's home. The only reason I haven't done so is because I'm angry at him for not stopping by when your new doctor came to Haven yesterday."

Her new doctor.

Dr. Anderson.

Noah.

Turning to face the bayou, Willa tried to hide her smile. The number of times Dr. Noah Anderson had entered her thoughts since their meeting had become too many to count.

But count them, she did.

And it was one hundred and thirty-six.

Lucy let out another lovesick sigh. "Do you think Paul has forgotten me?"

"It's all but agreed upon, Lucy."

"That's not what I'm asking."

"Any man who could forget you is not worth the worry," Willa said, deciding it was better to be honest than not. "I think it's time you let it be known that you're ready for him to stop dragging his feet."

Her sister beamed at the suggestion, looking as radiant as the sunset. Every so often, Willa could see traces of Grace in Lucy. "I think I will."

As they neared the rear of the house, the buzzing murmur of staff working below carried up on the wind, with Bonnie's voice ringing loudest of all.

"Bonnie is certainly in a tizzy tonight." With her hands on the concrete railing, Lucy leaned over the edge to have a peek. "Mother said she hired some Port Michaelson girls to come work in the kitchens. They're staying over through the winter to help get the house to rights after The Gathering and so we're running smoothly for the holidays."

That would explain the high-pitched giggling heard between Bonnie's orders. "Isn't that Jennie?" Willa joined Lucy in watching. They had never hired outsiders for such a long period. "The pretty one who brings the milk on Tuesdays?"

"You mean the one Cal can't take his eyes off whenever she comes around?" Lucy pointed to the group of four women currently being inspected by Bonnie on the lawn. "The very one."

"Oh, he's prowled around after her for at least two years, and now she's going to be here through the holidays?" Willa grinned at her sister. Their brother's reputation with women was quite improper for their ears, but the whispers made their way to them, nevertheless. "Perhaps The Gathering won't be so boring after all."

The Gathering was abysmal.

But not boring.

Standing on the stairs, Willa waved her satin hand-painted fan to circulate the stifling air and attempted to appear engaged with partygoers. She smiled here and inclined her head there, but thankfully, she was never required to converse.

John Richards arrived with his sister and with—miracle of miracles—nary a child in sight. Yet, when an hour passed, and he never made even the slightest bit of eye contact with her, too busy conversing with Lucy who had gone out of her way to be friendly with him, Willa began to think that perhaps the rumors weren't true.

And life as a spinster might be her fate after all.

Much to her mother's dismay, the Andersons arrived late, drawing the attention of the crowd. Willa wasn't at all surprised by the reaction. Not when dealing with a family such as the Andersons. Each more beautiful than the next, the lot was like nothing else in the area, and the arrival of Noah and his brother had only upped the ante. The trek to Haven House from both Hollingsdale and Port Michaelson wasn't easy, but it seemed that didn't matter. There were many Mamas in attendance tonight, all ready to thrust their eligible daughters into the fray.

It was like a pageant of the very best the county had to offer. Women of marriageable age filled the halls of Haven, ready to battle for the attention of Paul or poor Beau, who didn't quite know what to do with all the females surrounding him.

Not that Noah didn't have his fair share of attention. As a doctor, he came in last amongst the available men. Never to accumulate the fortune his cousin or brother would one day share, he was the least desirable of the lot, even if he was by far the most attractive.

In Willa's opinion, at least.

Cal was being sought after as much as the Anderson men. Watching from her perch, Willa snickered at the flock of girls following her poor brother from room to room as he himself chased after the serving girl, Jennie.

The entire affair gave a little humor to the evening. A distraction sorely needed. So much of a distraction that she didn't notice Noah's approach until he was right next to her.

"Would you like me to fetch you some punch?"

Startled by his arrival, Willa greeted him with a polite smile. "I'm fine, thank you."

"You don't look fine. You look bored." He matched her stance, wisely keeping two steps away with his own glass of punch in hand. "An angel watching over the debauchery below."

Willa released an unladylike snort. "This is Haven House, Dr. Anderson. Debauchery is not tolerated here."

"Yes, I know." He smiled, quite literally sending her heart racing. "I've met your mother."

Willa gripped the banister harder. The urge to get closer to him and lower herself to the next step had become quite alarming.

"May I call on you tomorrow?"

Her mouth fell open. In the entirety of her life, no man had ever requested to call on her. Partly because no men her age traveled as far as Haven House if they could help it, but mainly because she was just Willa. The plain, boring, sickly Fairweather girl who had nothing to offer.

And she knew he didn't mean it the way a normal man would. She wasn't a fool. She knew he meant to see her in a medical capacity, but as he watched her with a playful look in his eye, it was very difficult to remind her inner self of that fact.

At her silence, Noah continued to smile. Bigger, brighter, and beyond devastating. It was getting to the point where someone should truly say something to him about it. The man had no right to throw his charm around as he did.

"Why should you wish to call on me tomorrow?"

"To examine you?" His smile dimmed, and Willa said a little prayer of thanks. That infernal smile of his was a weapon. "I would like us to begin treatment as soon as possible, but I'll need to gather information, and since I'm finally settled, I was hoping we could start tomorrow. Privately."

The idea of being alone with him made her exceedingly nervous. She had already made a fool of herself once and didn't care to have a repeat performance so soon. "What kind of information?"

His gaze dipped, striking her mouth first before descending to sweep over her entire being. "The standard stuff. Height, heartbeat, and so on." Taking another step on the stairs, his eyes slowly returned to hers. "You do have a heartbeat, don't you, Ms. Fairweather?"

No, she most certainly did not. At least not in her chest. With him this close, her poor, weak heart had taken a dive straight into her stomach. Why bother with the exam? She was dead where she stood.

"Willa?"

And why did he always have to say her name like that? Husky and with a hint of familiarity. "Y-yes, I have a heartbeat."

Concern spiked in his gaze, wiping the amusement once there. "Are you feeling well?"

She cleared her throat. How much more embarrassing could this encounter become? And she was honestly growing tired of repeating *"I'm fine"* to nearly all his questions.

"I'm fine, Dr. Anderson."

"Are you lying to me, Ms. Fairweather?"

"Why would I lie to you?"

"Of that, I'm not sure." He brazenly moved to stand with her, sharing all the available space. "But if I am to help, lying to me is not advisable."

Impossible a feat as it seemed, Willa averted her gaze. His nearness was inappropriate and fraught with dangerous implications, should anyone notice.

"Dr. Anderson, please give me room to breathe."

"Does having people close cause you to feel out of breath?"

"No, of course not."

"Because if it did, the problem could be in your head," he replied, backing up to lean on the wall behind him. "An aversion to crowds can cause shortness of breath."

The party forgotten, Willa's head snapped to the man smugly sipping from one of her mother's good punch glasses. "I beg your pardon?"

"Ailments of the mind can be as debilitating as physical ones."

Willa blinked at him standing there, looking handsome in the candlelight. Her mother always kept Haven well-lit during The Gathering. There wouldn't be a dark corner or shadowed spot anywhere on the ground floor.

Yet in the flickering glow, shadows played across Noah Anderson's outrageously handsome face, giving him an almost sinister appearance. In truth, the dance of dark and light only increased his beauty, if a man could be called beautiful, and made her want to inch closer to see if he might truly be the devil in disguise.

"Are you implying that my lungs' inability to function properly is all in my head?" she asked casually as she fiddled with lace trim on her white kid gloves.

"It's happened before."

He waited as she mulled over his words, clearly not realizing that the debate going on in her mind had nothing to do with whether he was correct or not. Finally, after deciding not to hurl him and his implied diagnosis right down the stairs, Willa looked down her nose at him. "I am not upset by crowds, Dr. Anderson."

"Noah, if you please."

He was testing her. Gauging to see if her reaction was indeed from some unknown hysteria or, worse, from him.

"I would love to join in the festivities. To dance and engage with people I am not related to or even possibly have a conversation with a person who does not have fur."

He let out a short laugh. "Cats are not people."

"Well, they certainly converse better than most."

"Only because the conversation is one-sided."

It was her turn to squelch a smile. "Not true. Bonnie has a tabby who is quite vocal when he disapproves of something."

The noise in the hall grew in volume as the foremen from the mill arrived with their families. It was the one time of the year Stephen Fairweather permitted them admittance into his home.

Noah joined her at the banister. "A full house tonight," he remarked, his mouth entirely too close to her ear. "Will the mill workers arrive next?"

A heaviness settled in, his words carrying more weight than he realized. "The workers do not come anymore. Only the supervisors and their families are invited."

"Why don't the workers come?"

Willa turned to speak directly to him and sucked in a sharp slice of air, her head nearly knocking into his. He was close—too close—his face mere inches from hers. Not that she minded. He smelled delicious, and his jawline was still in need of a shave, the dark stubble making her wonder if it felt as rough as it looked. Maybe she might like to run her tongue across...

Tongue?

Good heavens.

Her spine snapped straight. What on earth was wrong with her?

"I'm going to be working with them," Noah went on as if the world hadn't tipped on its axis, knocking her off their earthly plane and straight into the pits of a harlot's hell. "My plan is to care for the mill workers until my time is up here. There's a small building between our property and yours, and I mean to utilize it. Although it will probably take me until I leave to get it sorted."

"That will be lovely," she replied, determined to keep her mind from wandering. "And needed."

Their gazes connected when he heard the tremor in her voice, and Willa imagined this was what it must feel like to stand on a mountaintop.

Dizzying heights and thin air, where the urge to jump feet first off a cliff became as loud as the heartbeat in your ears.

"Willa, are you positive you're alright?"

Why did his eyes continuously seek her mouth? Was there something on it? Had she not wiped all the cream from her lips after sneaking a pastry with Bonnie before retiring to her perch on the stairs?

"Willa?" His baritone voice had the hairs on her arms standing straight up. "Answer me."

She almost didn't, wanting to hear him say her name again. "I'm fine."

"Since you keep insisting that you're fine, even though you're breathless every time we speak," giving her room, he lowered himself to the step below, "then will you do me the honor of taking a turn about the party with me."

"Excuse me?" Oh, dear. That had come out louder than she expected. "Me?"

He was laughing at her again. "You don't mean to stand up here all night, do you?"

"I'm not permitted. Mr. Abernathy said I should avoid crowds."

One of his eyebrows, perfectly arched in severity, went up, and Willa learned very quickly that Dr. Noah Anderson did not care to be told no. "Mr. Abernathy?"

"The barber."

"The barber?"

"In Hollingsdale," she explained, knowing how ridiculous she sounded. "Father prefers that I see him rather than the woman who runs the apothecary. Mr. Abernathy isn't much to look at and only has two teeth left in his head, but he sincerely tries to help however he can."

Noah set his glass on the stair above, obviously trusting a staff member would whisk it away momentarily. "Ah, but you see, you're no longer in Mr. Abernathy's care, but in mine."

"Oh?"

"Yes, Wilhelmina Fairweather. You're mine to care for and mine to look after."

And there she was, back on that mountaintop and ready to jump.

"I can't."

She didn't know what to do with herself. Not when he straightened, nor when he offered his hand while smirking in a wicked way that had her feeling it right down to the tips of her toes.

"I hate to inform you, as you don't appear to be the type of woman who cares to hear such things, but you're wrong, Willa," he replied, leading her down the stairs together and into the main hall. "With me at your side, you can do anything."

CHAPTER 4

S he danced.

For the first time, Wilhelmina Fairweather danced in the ballroom of Haven House. It had been to a slow minuet, which she had taught herself how to do long ago with nothing more than an imaginary partner. Alone in her room, she had learned all kinds of dances, thinking there would never be an opportunity to show off her abilities.

Lying in bed, with the party over hours earlier, she smiled up at the ceiling as she relived every tiny detail of the evening.

The feel of her arm secured in Noah's muscular one.

The heat of his body as they made their way downstairs.

The shocked looks in the hall and the way the crowd parted to let them pass as if it were Moses himself escorting her to the promised land.

"Chin up, and eyes ahead," Noah had whispered when they made their way through the gauntlet of curious onlookers. "Don't let them see you afraid."

He meant her family. The disapproving glare of her mother could be felt like an arrow. Her father's stare, like an ax. Bonnie watched with concern, all of them afraid she would make a scene by having a breathing episode. Of course, if she did, then they would be required to act since they very well couldn't allow her to drop dead in the presence of guests.

Doing as Noah said, Willa found herself drawing strength from his belief in her. She couldn't ever recall another soul thinking that maybe, just maybe, she deserved to have a little fun without the worry of her lungs getting in the way.

And she did indeed have fun.

Entering the ballroom, the crowds continued to part. Her sister had been off in the corner, keeping Mr. Richards entertained. When Lucy saw them, she openly gasped in delight and even dragged Mr. Richards out to join in on the dance with her and Noah.

Noah.

Once the music played and the dance began, there had been nothing but him. In the full light of the candlelit ballroom, he had quite simply enchanted her with his charming nature. Most would call her melodramatic for saying such a thing, but it was true. Noah's charm radiated from within, seducing her with its power long after the party had ended.

Turning to her side, she cuddled into the pillow, sighing as heavily as Lucy had earlier in the evening. It was wrong to think of Noah like this. Nothing would become of her infatuation, and it would make their sessions together awkward.

But it didn't matter. As he escorted her back to that hellish spot on the stairs, Noah chatted and—in his own way—flirted. It had been a surprise, but once she reminded herself he was merely being kind, she relaxed, and their banter flowed. It turned out he was not totally set on leaving the area, debating between working for his family or returning north to open his own practice.

"The workers need available medical care, especially if there is an emergency, but I don't know that I'm the man for it," he'd said, lingering with her on the stairs long after the dance ended. "I enjoy the city. The noise. The people. Everyone is always in a hurry to get somewhere and nowhere all at once."

Willa admitted she didn't know of such things. "I've read about them... lived the lives of thousands of people through the pages of my books, but I'm sure I'll never experience it for myself."

"Never say never, Ms. Fairweather."

Never say never? Such faith he had.

In life.

In the future.

Probably because he had one.

Yawning, she listened to the pitter-patter of rain against her windows. Dawn was approaching, and while the wet season might be on its way out, the rumble of thunder and the violent flash of lightning across her windows told her that Mother Nature was setting the stage for yet another day inside Haven House.

No matter. In her mind, she danced again with Noah, the beat of their movements set to the downpour. He had been so attentive, acting as a proper dance partner should.

On their second dream waltz, her eyelids grew heavy, and she gave in to sleep, allowing it to whisk her into a world not her own. A place where she danced every dance and ran the streets of large cities with a trail of friends at her side.

Friends.

Friends were something she had never possessed. Her sisters were her confidants, the lifelines that kept her sane. Lucy functioned as her sounding board, but Grace... Grace had been Willa's everything. Gracious and kind, with a laugh that burrowed right into the heart, Grace was missed every second of the day.

A muffled thump startled Willa awake, and she lay in the dark for a moment, trying to discern where the noise had come from. No cats were in the room, and it didn't appear that Lucy had snuck in as she sometimes did when scared during a storm.

Another thump struck, more distinct than before, and Willa sat up, listening intently. It was coming from Grace's old bedroom next door, which was odd as no one used it. No one even entered it anymore. Seeing it empty was too painful, and only Bonnie went in to clean the cobwebs and dust every now and then.

When yet another knock hit the wall, Willa tossed her blankets aside and turned the lamp on her bedside table up to give the room light. The noise was most certainly coming from next door.

Tentatively, she went to the wall and placed her ear against it, thinking she was dealing with a group of wayward cats. If her mother found them upstairs making mischief in Grace's room, there would be hell to pay.

There was more shuffling, and with the side of her face pressed completely against the cold wall, a soft, feminine moan greeted her.

With a gasp, Willa straightened. No one would dare. No one. Not even a drunken party guest needing rest for the night would dare use Grace's room. They knew better. The eldest Fairweather daughter's absence continued to echo through the halls of Haven House, and to desecrate her private space would be unthinkable.

Another moan carried over, but then it transformed into...

Was that a giggle?

And singing?

Returning to press her ear to the wall again, she attempted to make out the words, but there were none. Just a sweet melody. One Willa had heard hundreds of times before and sung in the same manner.

"Grace?"

Impossible.

And yet.

She hurried over to where her robe hung, flinging it on like a mad woman to rush out. She didn't bother with her lamp, not needing light to guide her way to Grace's room. The full moon would do the job, illuminating the landing by shining through the large rear window facing the forest.

But on the landing, the singing stopped, and Willa stood barefoot, listening for more.

Across the landing, Lucy's door opened. "Willa?" she whispered. "What are you doing?"

"Did you hear singing?"

Bundling her own robe tighter, Lucy stepped out of her room. "Singing?"

"From Grace's room."

Lucy shrunk a little, sadness making her look like a small child. "Grace isn't singing, Willa."

She knew that, but...

"I heard her." Willa insisted. "I heard someone singing."

"Are you sure you weren't dreaming?"

Exasperated, Willa shushed her, thinking she might have heard it again. "Yes, I'm sure."

And there it was. The faint melody sung countless times by Grace.

Lucy heard it, too, and she paled in the ghostly moonlight. "Who is in there?"

They would never know, for as they darted in the direction of the singing, their mother's door began to open, and they were forced to retreat to their rooms quickly.

With her door locked and secured, Willa waited for signs of Margaret coming her way but heard nothing.

Nothing but the singing.

It was louder than before.

Lighter.

As if it were floating down from above.

Willa's chest pumped wildly in terror, and she remained cognizant of her breathing, but that wasn't saying much. A lion could be charging her in the wilds of Africa, and even then, she would remain cognizant of her breathing.

A pulse of lightning hit, illuminating the ceiling to reveal there was nothing up there.

And how ridiculous for her to think that there was. Of course, there was nothing up there. It must be Bonnie next door singing, for who else could it be?

A crash of thunder exploded, abruptly silencing the haunting song. Caught off guard, Willa stifled a scream and waited for it to pick up again.

But it never did.

CHAPTER 5

"Thank you for coming later in the day." Willa fidgeted nervously on the parlor's smaller sofa. "The entire household slept in after last night's festivities."

"As did ours," Noah replied, rummaging through the black leather bag he had brought with him. "Did you enjoy yourself last night?"

"I di—"

A crash in the hallway and Bonnie's harsh berating of the person responsible drowned out Willa's answer. "Stupid girl!" Bonnie shouted. "Watch what you're doing."

Willa rose from her sofa and closed the door, not exactly worried over the societal rules of propriety. If Noah were locked away with Lucy, it would be another story, but as it was only her, no one would be concerned.

"Sounds like everyone is a little tired today." Noah extracted an instrument and laid it on the table. "Or does your housekeeper usually not allow the staff to slip up from time to time."

"Bonnie isn't our housekeeper. She's more like my mother's personal companion. She's also very particular about how Haven House should be run. Even more so than Ms. Graham, our actual housekeeper." Willa returned to her seat, slightly nervous over what to expect from him today.

"And what you heard was Bonnie scolding some Port Michaelson girls who were hired to help with The Gathering. I hear the plan is to have them stay on through the holidays, so Bonnie is likely just getting them up to snuff on how she expects things done."

Noah's profile was to her, and the wry smile on his lips dimmed slightly. "Yes, I met a few of them last night."

"The Port Michaelson girls?"

"Those are the ones."

Willa released a noise that clearly expressed how unimpressed she was by his tone, and even though it might seem a bit pathetic for her to be jealous, that didn't change the fact that she was.

Smoothing a hand down the skirt of her mossy green afternoon dress, Willa got ahold of herself. "The one named Jennie is the prettiest. My brother falls all over himself whenever she comes by with deliveries."

"I noticed her."

"It's hard not to." She tried to sound flippant and slightly bored. It wasn't working. "Notice her, I mean."

Turning around, the half-smirk that seemed permanently affixed to his mouth returned. "How was your conversation with Richards?"

Lucy had brought John Richards over twice, and both times were unmemorable. They spoke little, with him chatting more with her sister than with her.

"Lovely."

"It didn't appear lovely to me."

"And I didn't realize I had an audience."

Amused by her quick reply, he came to sit on the sofa with her, taking up a significant amount of space. "If a man is near you, Willa, you should always assume you have an audience."

If her brows shot up any faster, they would have flown right off her head and across the room. "I don't know what you mean."

And she didn't. Truly. No man who had entered the kingdom of Haven House ever paid her attention. Nor had any man who she interacted with on visits to town.

His insinuation bordered on teasing, and Willa's guard went up. Being ridiculed constantly by her father required her defenses to be at the ready every second of the day, and those well-worn walls of self-preservation slid into place easily.

Noah hesitated before speaking again. "I mean that it is difficult for a man's attention not to gravitate towards a woman like you."

"A woman like me?" Her temper snapped its teeth, preparing to take a bite out of him. "An invalid looming on the stairs, you mean."

His smirk evaporated. "That's not what I meant."

"Isn't it?" Chin high, she wouldn't allow him to see how deeply his words cut. "Why else would any man—"

"You *can't* be serious."

"—be drawn to watch—"

"You *are* serious."

"—a woman like me."

He laughed.

Loudly.

It burst right out of him, booming as forcefully as the thunder had in the night. She tried to ignore it and keep a straight face rather than sigh over how his eyes crinkled in their corners when he was happy.

"I will have you stop laughing at me now, Dr. Anderson."

The mischief in his gaze lingered, but he quieted. "I'm not laughing at you, but at me."

When she didn't respond, the gleam in those imposing blue eyes of his turned dark, almost predatorial. It reminded her of the look Bonnie's cats got when there was easy prey within reach.

"And why are you laughing at yourself?"

Arranging the stethoscope in his ears, he placed the receiving end on her chest without warning or permission. One moment, he was sitting straight, and the next, he was leaning precariously close.

"Because it's been so long since I've paid a woman a compliment, it would appear that I no longer have the finesse for it as I once did." His brows snapped together, a frown overtaking him while he listened. "Your heartbeat sounds rather erratic. Are you feeling alright?"

"Don't do that."

Yanking one of the earpieces of the stethoscope loose, he scanned her quickly. "You're not alright, are you?"

His concern was shattering, heartbreaking to a dizzying degree. It was his profession—to care, to treat, to want her to be at her best.

But with his confession of genuinely paying her a compliment, Willa had been swiftly whisked into a place she dare not ever tread. An enchanting false reality where a man such as Noah Anderson would see her as something other than a fragile enigma. That he would see her as a woman. Not a problem, not a bother, nor even a burden to be rid of, but as a woman. A woman he wanted to pay a compliment to.

"For the hundredth time, I'm fine, Dr. Anderson."

"Noah, please."

She shook her head stupidly, so very lost in the possibilities staring back at her. He could never be Noah again. It was to be Dr. Anderson forever. The formality made the relationship as it should be. Doctor and patient. To now call him Noah—to have his given name on her lips—would be torture for sure. Using his given name would provide her with a sick sense of hope, and if there was one thing she knew for sure, it was that hope had no place at Haven House.

It had no place with her.

After the dances, she had obviously fooled herself into believing he was merely being kind. But this openly flirtatious side of him would be her downfall. Death by means of a handsome face.

"I was taken aback by the stethoscope." She turned away, patting her loosely braided bun as if it were going to come undone due to her lack of composure. "Mr. Abernathy's is nothing like the one you have."

Pulling it completely loose, he held it out for her to see. "Try it."

"I'd rather not."

"I insist. The last thing I want is for you to feel uneasy with my instruments."

Beyond the parlor's front windows, Cal and Lucy caught her attention. They were talking on the porch, brother and sister, in the afternoon sun. Happy. They looked so very happy. A golden pair enjoying the fading warmth of the day.

The hope she was already attempting to squash died as she watched her siblings. They had their whole lives ahead of them while she had nothing. "Your instruments do not disturb me, Dr. Anderson. I've been poked and prodded by more nefarious things. A stethoscope is a toy in comparison."

Settling back on the cushions, he observed Cal and Lucy with her. "Tell me about it."

"There's nothing much to tell." Willa smiled as Lucy threw her head back, laughing at something Cal said. She looked like Grace just then, reminding her, and likely Cal, of happier times. "I promise you that my stories are boring."

"Oh, I highly doubt that."

"And why do you doubt it?"

"Because they're yours."

Clever man. But two could play his game. "I was born. I grew up."

"Do you mean to quote me Dickens, Ms. Fairweather?"

"Be sure to visit Haven House at Christmastime, Dr. Anderson." She smiled serenely, masking the pain as she continued to bury it from the light as she always did. "Everyone gathers to hear me read *A Christmas Carol* aloud. I've been told I'm positively riveting."

He regarded her quietly for a moment, then replied with a serious tone, "Yes, but do you change your voice for the different characters? Only a true storyteller would."

"Oh, yes, and I also have wardrobe pieces, thank you very much."

"Good." He returned his stethoscope to his ears, feigning professionalism once again. "I would expect nothing less from Wilhelmina Fairweather."

He spoke as if they had been acquainted for ages. As if they had known each other through the ups and downs of their journey. Surprisingly, it did feel that way.

And she really knew nothing about him.

"I've told you my story, Dr. Anderson." Willa held still as he listened to her heart, praying it had returned to a normal rhythm. "Let's hear yours."

"You've given me very little, Ms. Fairweather." He straightened and wrote something down in the notebook perched on his thigh. His very *muscular* thigh. "But since it seems you've mastered the art of deflecting, I suppose I'll take pity on you."

He was annoyed by her lack of elaboration on the treatments she'd received but was too much of a gentleman to push. The contrast intrigued her. "Do tell."

"I was born..."

It was her turn to laugh openly. "Are you mocking me?"

"Most certainly," he replied. "Now, open your mouth."

It was always the same thing. They wanted to see if there was something constricting her throat. A growth in the inner lining of the mouth. Anything they could attribute her breathing issues to other than asthma.

"In addition to Mr. Abernathy, I saw two physicians when I was younger, and they also checked my mouth and throat. There's nothing there. I have asthma, and that is all."

He stared at her, his eyes narrowing as if she were between the hairs of a crossbow. The doctor very much did not like being told no. "Open your mouth, please."

"I assure you I have a completely normal—"

He gripped her chin, catching her off guard once more. "*Open* for me."

The demand gave no room for thought, nor did his strong fingers forcing her jaw open. Eyes wide, and taken aback, she obeyed. There was no fighting, no fussing. The muscles in her jaw simply went lax, opening for him as ordered.

"Ah, is that how it's to be?" His deep voice dropped an octave, and scanning her throat, his tongue darted out to lick his lips. "I think you take great joy in being contradictory."

The swipe of his tongue across that perfectly formed full bottom lip nearly had Willa groaning. The movement was so very chaste, yet the most carnal thing she had ever witnessed. A throbbing heat speared low in her belly, and she squirmed, unable to hold still.

"But if that's how you wish to proceed with our sessions, then I am ready and more than capable of rising to the challenge," he continued, this time grazing his teeth over said lip. "In fact, I feel as though I might rather enjoy it." His gaze rose slowly to meet her own. "I think you will, too."

Staring at him, something tugged at the heart buried deep in her chest. It burned hot and fast, the pressure of its heat squeezing her very soul.

Noah released his hold on her chin. "Don't you agree?"

Agree?

Agree to what?

"Y-yes?" she stammered, wondering what in the world was wrong with her. Overheated. Yes, that must be it. She had simply become overheated while he examined her throat. Obviously, it was stifling in the room since Noah—Dr. Anderson—removed his coat directly upon arriving, and the heat was going straight to her head.

"Good." Rising from the sofa, Noah returned to his bag left propped on one of the parlor's end tables. "You have a small amount of scar tissue in the back of your throat. Can you tell me how that happened?"

"No?" She swallowed, not feeling anything. "I would often choke on my food when I was little, and then the whole episode would go straight into a breathing attack. Mr. Abernathy told me it was there, even though I don't feel it. He said it was probably from overexerting myself while coughing."

Noah made a rumbling noise, and she couldn't tell if the sound meant that he agreed with the assessment or not. "Do you have scars anywhere else on your body?" he asked.

"No?" Why did she sound so unsure? It was her blasted body, and she would know if there were scars somewhere. "No."

"Hmm, perhaps I should conduct a more thorough examination. We might need to bring your mother in to chaperone for this next part."

Good heavens.

"Is that type of exam really necessary?"

"Yes, I think so."

Willa nearly shouted in relief when Lucy barged in waving a piece of paper. "Mr. Richards is coming for a visit!"

"Why?" It was a stupid question. Willa knew exactly why. She had made the short list of possible wives. "I mean, when?"

"Father just received word." Winded, Lucy paused to catch her breath. "In two days. He's going to spend the afternoon with us."

The zipper on Noah's bag zinged closed with such finality that both she and Lucy turned to him. "I'm also scheduled to return in two days for a follow-up," he said.

Lucy's face fell. "Well, surely you can come on a different day?"

"Today was about gaining baseline measurements on your sister's overall health, but there is much more work to do."

Assessing the abrupt change in him, Willa tilted her head. If she didn't know any better, she would think he was jealous. "And what do you plan to do with me, Dr. Anderson?"

Noah fixed his gaze on her. "I mean to test your limits, Ms. Fairweather. I hope you're ready."

CHAPTER 6

"The tapestry in the hall comes from the Fairweather ancestral home all the way in Scotland," Lucy said, pouring tea to serve John Richards. "It's rather ugly, if you ask me."

Willa smiled politely, waiting for John to speak, but he had yet to do so—at all. In the full hour that had passed since his arrival, she had received only a nod in greeting.

Through this entire ordeal, her saving grace had been Lucy. Her sister played the part of hostess beautifully, and Willa wished Paul Anderson was here to see it. The stupid man had hardly paid Lucy any attention at The Gathering, too busy watching the local girls with Cal.

"We have another one in the dining room," Willa said, attempting to participate in the conversation. "Lucy, do you remember the time Cal almost caught it on fire when we were younger?"

"Oh, yes!" Lucy took a seat next to Mr. Richards, keeping a proper distance. They didn't often have male callers at Haven House, but both she and Lucy had been trained to a fault on how to behave. "And he would have caught the entire dining room on fire if not for Grace coming to save the day."

When Grace was mentioned in public, she and Lucy's lightness dimmed—it always did.

"Grace is your sister?" John asked, sipping at his tea. "I've heard of her."

Of course, he had. The entire county had heard of Grace. A beauty with wit and brains, the eldest Fairweather daughter had once been the most sought-after prize for miles.

"Is she happy?" John asked, lowering his voice. The door to the parlor had been left wide open, and the man was smart enough to know that there were eyes and ears everywhere in this house. "You don't have to tell me if you do not wish, but whatever her reasons were for running off with him, I hope it was worth it and that she's happy."

Willa did too, but God was the only one who would know for sure.

"Yes," Willa replied, thinking it best to leave it at that. "Tell me, Mr. Richards, how are your children?"

She wanted to completely understand what she might be getting herself into. She had never entertained the idea of children because she couldn't. From as far back as she could remember, every individual who ever treated her had warned against having them.

But she might like them—a built-in family at the ready. It wouldn't be easy, not with the children having lost their mother a year ago, but perhaps she might find herself falling into the role with ease.

"My little Clara has lost her first tooth." With a soft smile, John tried to make eye contact with her but failed and spoke to Lucy as if she had been the one to ask the question. "It was quite the scene. My oldest son, Christopher, tried to help. It ended well, but children are children."

The fondness in his voice told Willa this might not be so bad after all. John Richards held genuine affection for his family, a foreign concept to Fairweathers to be sure, but it spoke more for him than any other recommendation.

"Am I correct in thinking that your youngest is not yet two years old?" Willa asked. "That must be quite a feat to raise all those children on your own and manage the farm."

"The older children help." He set his teacup on the end table, a nervous tremor in his hands. John Richards married his wife when they were both terribly young, and this courting business was likely just as nerve-wracking for him as it was for Willa. "I have a staff as well. We might be a small farmhouse, but it's large enough to maintain one."

This meant she would have a household to run. Nothing similar to Haven House, but it sounded like enough to occupy her time.

"Then we have the farm hands," John continued. "There are seven in total, rotating between the livestock and crops."

Livestock?

She was going to have to manage children *and* a household *and* livestock?

Lucy appeared absolutely enthralled. "You mentioned at The Gathering how you have a large pasture. What kind of animals do you keep there?"

A knock at the parlor entrance interrupted her sister, and Willa's heart jumped into her throat when she saw Noah standing in the doorway. With a fresh shave, his hair swept back from his face and dressed in a form-fitting coat and vest that hugged his muscled frame perfectly, the man looked ready to devastate every female within miles.

"Are you ready for me, Ms. Fairweather?"

"Dr. Anderson!" Lucy and John rose to stand. "Won't you join us? We were just having tea with Mr. Richards."

Willa remained seated, too stunned by his appearance to move. She had been expecting him later and thought there would at least be time to have tea with John Richards before Noah arrived to turn her into a befuddled fool.

"I would love to." Entering, Noah set his bag on a side table before shaking John's hand. "I can do it myself, Lucy," he said when Lucy attempted to pour him tea. "I've spent many long nights in Philadelphia having to make do with just myself."

Willa narrowed her eyes. He was up to something.

"Is that where you studied?" Lucy asked, nervously watching the parlor door and Noah as he poured. Should their mother unexpectedly enter, Margaret would not be pleased to see a guest serving themselves. "In Philadelphia?"

"It is, and I enjoyed my time there." Noah took over the wingback next to Willa. He was so very tall, and the piece of furniture looked positively miniature under him. "Tell me, Mr. Richards. When I came in, I heard the mention of livestock. What type of animals do you have?"

"I was just asking that same question." Lucy nodded earnestly as she returned to her seat. "Cows?"

"I do have a cow or two," John replied. "Chickens, of course. Pigs, goats, and the like."

"Goats?" Noah said, taking a sip of his tea. "Hmm."

Willa's head swiveled in his direction. She was becoming accustomed to those little noises he made before unleashing some sort of shocking statement or observation.

Noah spared her a glance. "Have you ever been around goats, Willa? Their fur can set off asthma attacks. We studied a woman who dissolved into fits whenever around them."

"I have not," she replied tersely, hating him for ruining this small moment of normalcy. It wasn't every day she had tea in the parlor with a gentleman caller who had no interest in listening to the way she breathed. "But I am sure I will be fine."

Noah returned his attention to John Richards. "Are you aware of Willa's breathing issues?"

If he had doused her in kerosene and set her aflame, Willa would have been less surprised. And less furious. He had no right. Everyone knew of her disorder, but no one had the gall to speak about it openly with a person who was essentially a stranger. "Now is not the time to discuss such things," she snapped. "We were having a lovely conversation before your arrival."

The devil was amused, the corners of his lips curving upward as he sampled the tea again. "I think Mr. Richards will agree with me in that any information regarding your well-being remains a *lovely* topic of conversation."

Willa now understood why Haven's female cats attacked their male counterparts so often. "Well, I do not wish to discuss it."

"What would you rather us discuss?" Noah shot back. "How much you loved dancing at The Gathering, yet I was the only one who asked?"

"No, I would not." Willa reminded herself not to snarl. "I would like to hear about..."

Everyone waited expectantly, and as her mouth opened and closed like a fish out of water, her brain decided it was a good time to send the first thing it thought of out of her mouth and into the world.

"Pigs." Dash it all, she could never handle being under pressure, but there was no going back. "Are they truly clean animals?"

Lucy's eyes went as round as the saucer on which her teacup rested while Noah choked on his laughter.

"They are," John confirmed, seeming to relax. "Pigs only roll in the mud to keep cool."

"Do they overheat easily?" Willa asked, making this positively horrifying conversation worse. "And do they truly eat anything?"

"They overheat no more than a normal animal, and yes, they do eat anything." John nodded enthusiastically, obviously a connoisseur of pigs. "Even people."

Lucy popped open her fan, flapping it rapidly. Discussions regarding farm animals and their eating habits were not a topic covered during the social lessons provided by their mother and Bonnie.

"Are you overheating, Lucy?" Noah asked, hiding his smile. "Shall we roll you around in the mud like one of Mr. Richards' pigs?"

"No, I am most certainly not." Lucy stood abruptly to march over to the tea cart. "It is a lovely day."

Willa sighed. It really was going to be a nice day. The first of its kind in months. The temperature outside remained warm, but the afternoon breeze held a crisper tone, signaling that her beloved dry season would arrive soon.

"I want to use the lack of dampness in the air to our advantage," Noah agreed, rising to join Lucy at the cart. "What say you and I take

Willa and Mr. Richards for a walk outside?" He nudged her shoulder good-naturedly, clearly trying to make amends for intruding. "I'm sure Mr. Richards enjoys the outdoors, and Willa looks as if she needs some fresh air."

Lucy giggled, utterly charmed by him. "I think that sounds splendid."

"Explain to me why I am being paraded through the woods on your arm when this entire afternoon was arranged for Mr. Richards and myself to become better acquainted."

Not answering, Noah maneuvered them around a gnarled root protruding from the ground. The forest path between the Anderson estate and Haven House was full of them thanks to an overabundance of cypress trees in the area.

Several feet ahead, Lucy and John walked together, their heads close as they talked.

"Poor Lucy has probably learned more about pigs than she ever wanted to know," Willa whispered. "I might not be able to breathe correctly, but she has a weak stomach."

Noah tried to hide his grin but was doing a horrible job of it. "I've always found this trail to be lovely."

Willa rolled her eyes. Since the four of them stepped out onto Haven's porch, and Noah insisted she walk with him so he could study her breathing patterns, it had been one casual remark about nature after another.

"It's a wonder there's not more wildlife around, but I suppose the mills keep them away."

"Oh, will you stop," she hissed, only making his grin grow. "You don't give a flip about trees or animals."

"Not true, Ms. Fairweather." Noah schooled his features, suddenly taking a serious tone. "I'm quite fond of goats."

"You're a beast unto yourself, Dr. Anderson."

"Undoubtedly."

Lucy glanced back at them. "Is it much farther, Noah?"

Noah aimed a smile at her sister, and Willa did the same, not wanting anyone to know she was plotting the murder of a certain physician. "Just around the bend," he called out to her. "Two more curves on the trail, and we should be there."

They were walking the half-mile eastern path toward the building Noah was planning to use as a clinic. He claimed he wanted Willa to know where to find him if she ever needed him.

"Are you at all winded?" he asked softly. "We can slow down and allow them to go ahead."

"I'm doing well and thankful to be out of the house."

And she truly was enjoying the late afternoon sun. Gathering her embroidered cashmere shawl around her shoulders, she thought that perhaps they could visit the satsuma grove behind Haven once they finished at Noah's cottage.

Thinking of the grove, Willa remembered she wanted to ask Bonnie if anyone had warned the Port Michaelson girls about the manchineel trees growing along the water near the mill. They wouldn't want them to be taking a walk through the trails and accidentally mistake a manchineel for an apple.

"How often are you able to get fresh air?" Noah asked.

A group of birds flitted about overhead in the canopy, and she smiled wistfully at the sign of life. The cover of trees here was not as thick as the one over the trails leading to their mill and family graveyard.

"The air around Haven House is hardly ever fresh, thanks to the mills," she replied. "I do better without the damp air, so I would say I can roam freely outdoors for about two months out of the year."

"You deserve the sun every single day of your life, Willa." He looked as if he wanted to say more but shook his head. "I want you to be able to get out more."

He felt sorry for her, which was a shame because she had stopped feeling sorry for herself long ago. A single human could only live with so much regret before it began to eat away at their soul. "I am thankful for days like today. Others who suffer with my condition have it far worse, or so I hear."

"Some do, but they tend to change the environmental aspects that cause them to fall into attacks."

"What do you mean?"

Slowing their pace, Noah kept his gaze trained on the back of Lucy and John's heads. "If a goat is causing you to be unable to breathe, what would you do with the goat?"

"Get rid of it."

"Exactly. You have too many goats in your world."

"Goats?"

"Yes, goats."

Willa wrinkled her nose at him. "I'm afraid I don't follow, Dr. Anderson."

"Get rid of the goats," he grated, with an annoyed growl in his tone. "And will you please start calling me Noah?"

"I'm going to start calling you Dr. Goat since you seem mildly obsessed with them," Willa grumbled. "Then again, at least you're not enthralled with pigs, so I suppose I shouldn't complain."

A pair of squirrels, lost in the throes of courtship, scampered out of the woods. Round and round in a circle they went until the male of the pair nearly caught his female prey.

Too busy watching the fluffy-tailed rodents, Willa tripped on an exposed root. As the ground rushed up to greet her face, she gasped when it never connected.

Having swiftly caught her before impact, Noah set her to rights by wrapping her in his arms. Standing together, neither moved, the two of them blinking at one another while the squirrels disappeared to continue their dance up a nearby oak.

"I-I'm very sorry." Pressed against his chest, Willa's mind could only comprehend the hard muscle holding her upright. He was so very large, unyieldingly male, and like nothing else she had ever touched in her life. "Truly, sorry."

Somewhat aware that Lucy and Mr. Richards had taken the trail's curve already and were no longer within sight, Willa remained in her spot, wanting to linger in his arms.

And Noah made no move to release her.

"The goats," he exhaled as Willa stared at him, completely fascinated. Not by the goats, but by the small flecks of green mixing with the blue of his irises. This close, they were dazzling in the sunlight, the tiny imperfections making him more human yet all the more alluring. "You have to remove the goats, Willa."

Noah Anderson had to be the most beautiful man in creation. A specimen for all others of his sex to live up to. But, *good heavens*, the man was surprisingly horrid at getting his point across.

Not that she could comprehend much in her current situation.

"I don't have any goats."

His eyes dropped to her lips, and she didn't mind so much this time around. The slow progression of his gaze charged the very air as if a lightning strike were imminent—a bolt of electricity to match the emotions coursing through her.

"The goats are an analogy." His throat worked as he swallowed, chest rising and falling with every word. "You must get rid of what is setting off your attacks."

"Well, it's safe to say that it's not goats as I've never been around one," she joked, trying to break the magic of the moment and stall yet another heartbreak waiting to happen. "They don't appear to be creatures I would get along with at all."

"Are you sure?" Noah broke out into a grin. An honest to God one that struck her directly in the stomach. "They're very stubborn."

"I am not stubborn."

"Yes, you are, but rest assured, you are much more beautiful than a goat."

She couldn't stop herself from laughing. "Do you always compare the women you find beautiful to farm animals, Dr. Anderson?"

As her smile grew, his faded, dissolving into a thin line. His gaze once fixed on her mouth, roamed over her face, seeking every imperfection—the freckles, the pale skin, that obnoxious *beauty* mark along her jaw. He took it all in with equal parts awe and wonderment as if he had discovered some rare creature in the forests of Haven House.

"Wilhelmina Fairweather, you are much more than beautiful," he whispered. "You're extraordinary."

Her heart sank. His compliment did nothing more than remind her of the pathetic life she lived every day. "I don't want to be extraordinary. I want to be like you and Lucy and even boring John Richards."

At the mention of John Richards, his hold lessened, and she stepped forward, not willing to let it end. Not yet. Dear universe, let her have just a second more of his touch.

"Never underestimate the stability that comes from being ordinary," she continued. "I want to ride a horse on a hot, windy day. I want to run—truly run—on the sandy shore that is but a mile from my home. I want to understand what it means to take joy in the simple things because those simple things, while ordinary to you and others," she released a humorless laugh, "are not so simple for me."

The large hand splayed upon her back moved forward to capture her wrist. It stalled there, his thumb grazing back and forth over the hammering pulse beating against her skin. "Well, now you've gone and done it, Ms. Fairweather."

She really should have extracted herself from his hold by now, but she couldn't find the want or strength to do so. "And what is that, Dr. Anderson?"

Noah drew a long breath, and looked down at where he held her wrist. "Provided me with a new purpose in life."

The sun peeked out from behind the clouds, and rays of sunshine streamed through the canopy, dancing with the branches and leaves fluttering in the afternoon breeze. Tipping his face to the sky, Noah closed his eyes to bask in the light.

"A new purpose?" The question squeaked out of her, and she attempted to strengthen her voice and make it less breathy. "Such as what, exactly?"

"Wiiillllaaaaa." Lucy's singsong voice carried over to them through the forest. "Are you coming?"

The spell over, Noah released his hold and placed her arm in his without answering. Unsure of what to do or say as they continued on the path in silence, Willa's mind raced with thought on what just happened. A new purpose? What could he have possibly meant?

"Wiiiilllllaaaa."

"We're coming, Lucy," she shouted so her sister could hear. "No need to sing. I think we've had enough of that lately."

They were nearing the curve on the path and would run into Lucy and Mr. Richards at any moment. "Are you not fond of singing?" Noah asked. "Are you all Shelly and Dickens with no heart to it?"

She wasn't sure what had happened back there, but a shift had taken place, something between them changing. "I love singing. It's only that Lucy and I were awakened by someone singing in the middle of the night."

"Who on earth would be singing in the middle of the night?" he asked, cocking an eyebrow. "No, wait. I know. It's your mother, isn't it? At her heart, she's a truly passionate soprano."

A whoop of laughter loud enough to frighten every animal around burst from Willa. "No, Dr. Anderson."

"Your father, then?"

It wouldn't stop—the laughter, the ludicrousness of the idea tickling her brain as she imagined her father belting out a tune.

Smug by his ability to make her happy, Noah smirked at the path ahead. "Careful with all that laughter, Ms. Fairweather. I wouldn't want you to overextend yourself on my watch."

"Oh, I am quite sure that is a lie." Willa regained control of herself, although barely. "I imagine you would love me to overextend myself just so you can poke and prod me with the things you keep stored in that black bag of yours."

He made a noise low in his throat but didn't comment. "So, who was doing the singing?"

"It was likely Bonnie. She once sang all the time but hasn't since…" She paused, unsure of which story had been told to him. "Since my sister Grace lived at Haven House."

They rounded the turn, carefully stepping over a large fallen branch on the path. Straight ahead, Lucy and Mr. Richards waited next to what could only be described as a cottage. Small and worn, the old place had seen better days.

"I thought there were only three of you?"

Ah, so Noah had not yet been told of the Fairweather family scandal. Willa watched her sister laughing over something Mr. Richards said. They were too far off to make out the conversation, but the pair appeared to be getting along nicely. "Grace is the oldest."

"Does she live in Hollingsdale?"

"No," Willa replied and nodded at the house. "You've got your work cut out for you."

"It will take some time to organize," Noah agreed, suddenly looking almost boyish as he rubbed a hand on the back of his neck. "It's a perfectly sound building, though. Once I have a few things in order, I plan to stay late every night to get it ready. I might even need to sleep over instead of trying to make it back to my uncle's home in the middle of the night. I wouldn't want to get attacked by some nocturnal animal looking for its next meal."

On her left, something in the brush moved. A slight imbalance in the autumn air. A shadow that wanted Willa to look.

To see.

To remember.

As if she could forget.

She ignored it, too scared to acknowledge its presence.

And so, it followed, watching and listening. Its curiosity about Noah working as a reminder for Willa not to become too attached.

"Yes, you should be careful in these woods at night, Dr. Anderson." Willa forced a smile that would fool any man alive. A carefully practiced one every Fairweather woman knew how to do. "There are things more dangerous than animals lurking about."

CHAPTER 7

"And why is that doctor coming yet again?"

Eyes forward and sitting as straight as they possibly could, Cal was the only one who dared answer their father. "Noah comes every two to three days and has since The Gathering."

"But why?" Stephen Fairweather might have been keen on manners for his children and had even higher expectations of his wife, but he held no such regard for himself. Sitting at the head of the massive mahogany dining room table, he chewed with his mouth open, glaring at Willa as she fought not to squirm. "Hasn't he fixed you yet, girl?"

One of the logs in the fireplace cracked like a gunshot, and Willa nearly jumped out of her skin, already a jumble of nerves under her father's scrutiny. "No, sir. Not as of yet."

"Imagine that." Her father's beady eyes assessed her, likely seeking a weak spot to strike and make it hurt. "It's been a month."

A month. Thirty days. All of it passing in a whirl as she spent time with Noah. He came three times a week, maybe more, if not busy treating the ailments and injuries of those working at the mills. Together in the library, they would discuss books and life. He would tell her of his travels, which he insisted were not grand but still held Willa in rapt attention.

Noah had seen and done so much in his twenty-eight years of life—much more than she would ever do in the entirety of hers.

Of course, their talks also included ways to treat her condition. He had written to a friend in Ohio, a doctor who specialized in breathing ailments. Noah said the man would send them tea leaves to try during her next attack.

"The leaves come from a plant indigenous to South America and can be chewed or brewed into a tea you can sip on during an episode," he had explained. "I've seen it in action, and it can honestly work if we catch the oncoming attack early enough."

Calling on all her courage, Willa replied to her father, "Dr. Anderson is working through the information I've given him."

"And what of Mr. Richards?" he barked, his fork scraping against the plate as he stabbed at the slab of meat there. "Why is John Richards not coming to visit?"

"Um, the bridge?"

Willa scrambled to explain what her father already knew. A piece of the bridge that connected Hollingsdale to Haven's section of earth had been washed out during a horrific fall storm. It occurred a few days after John Richards came for tea, and while the repairs were scheduled to be completed next week, they had yet to hear when he would be calling on her again.

"He could have taken the ferry like everyone else." Her father shoveled more food into his mouth. "There is nothing about you that is even remotely appealing, and you must work harder than other women to obtain a man. Show him that you're interested, or he will forget you."

"Letters." The single word slipped from her mother's lips. "John Richards and Willa exchange letters."

Willa refused to glance at Lucy, the true mastermind behind the letters. When her mother demanded that she begin writing to John Richards, Willa had drawn a blank, relying on Lucy to fill the space with more elegant prose. John's replies came quickly, with one or two a day arriving at a steady pace.

"How romantic, Willa." Cal sneered, eating along with their father while no one else did. "Has he confessed his love for you yet?"

"No," she answered through clenched teeth. "But I'm sure it's coming any day now."

"Let us hope," Cal said from his seat beside their father. He always sat to the left, with Bonnie forever assigned to sit at Stephen Fairweather's right. Willa, her mother, and Lucy were long ago banished to the farthest end of the table, or as they liked to call it, the wasteland of the unwanted. "Those acres of Richards are perfect for our future endeavors."

Their father grunted, hunched over his plate as he finished his meal. "Good planting land."

"Good building land, too," Cal countered. "We could build an estate twice the size of Haven House on it and wi—"

Their father's hand smacked the table, the plates rattling under the force of the hit. "Enough of that talk. I won't hear it."

Willa froze and waited with her mother and Lucy, the three of them understanding to keep silent. Silent and still *or else*.

"This is our land." Her father's finger stabbed the table. Punctuated again by the rattle of cutlery and porcelain. "This is our home."

Another stab.

"Haven House belongs to the Fairweathers and us to it." Leaning forward to speak directly in his son's face, Stephen Fairweather hissed the same promise he uttered every time Cal brought up the idea of relocating to Hollingsdale. "I. Will. Never. Leave. This. Place."

"Perhaps you won't." Unafraid, Cal met their father's gaze head-on, his own uncompromising nature matching that of the man who sired him. "But I don't want to spend my life here. I'll run the lumber mill, but we don't have to live so close."

Willa imagined everyone at the table suddenly knew how she felt when a breathing attack struck. The air in the room simply vanished, sucked in sharply by all those present. From the corner of her eye, she saw Bonnie incline her head at the two serving girls standing quietly against the wall.

They were part of the Port Michaelson set and hurried from the room without further instruction.

Stephen Fairweather watched the young women go, his wandering eye for Haven's female staff nothing new. Neither was his love of the drink, and snatching up his cup, he downed the remainder of the noon-day wine as if it were water.

And only once the twelve-foot dining hall doors creaked closed behind the Port Michaelson girls did their father speak. "It doesn't matter what you want. It matters what I want."

Cal's upper lip curled in disgust, his gaze sweeping over the remains of food and drink spilled across the front of their father's clothes. "But what if John Richards doesn't want Willa?" he asked. "The marshland across the sound is only deepening, and our groves continue to suffer. If we have no harvest, we have no mill, and without other avenues of income to fall back on, we'll lose."

Blotches of red broke out across their father's face. One at a time, growing larger and larger until he resembled an overripe apple. Next to Willa, her mother struggled. Margaret might be a terror to her children, but at times like this, when their sanity during the upcoming holidays hung in the balance, the venom she usually sputtered dried up.

Only one person at the table could diffuse the situation.

"Stephen."

Their story was no secret to the family. Stephen Fairweather, the sinner. Bonnie Sikes, the saint. The tale of a wretched man's heartless ways chasing him into the long years of his life.

"The boy has been to school and gained fantastical ideas," Bonnie said while father and son continued to glare at each other. She looked lovely today, dressed in a handsome burgundy tea dress instead of her usual dowdy wrapper and apron. Her dark brown hair was styled as well, drawn up into a neat coiffure with rolls and plaits that only her slender fingers could manage. "You should listen and be proud that Calvin is looking for ways to improve your family's fortune."

If an outsider ever heard household staff members speak to an employer in such a way, they would be appalled. Outraged beyond belief. Yet where Margaret Fairweather lacked the talent to reason with her husband, her faithful companion excelled at it. And why shouldn't she?

Bonnie had nearly a lifetime of practice.

"The mill is our future, Bon." The reddening in his cheeks lessened, and Willa exhaled slowly as her father poured himself more wine. "You know it, and I know it."

"I also know times are changing," Bonnie said, laying her hand on his. "Who are we to argue with the changing times?"

Her father spared a glance at the tiny woman he respected more than anyone else. "Indeed."

Sweethearts.

They had been sweethearts growing up.

Not only did the entire county know how Stephen Fairweather preferred to bed serving girls rather than his own wife, but they also remembered the time he had once fallen madly in love with one of them. A pretty kitchen maid named Bonnie, who loved him in return. It had been quite a scandal, and when forced to give her up and marry a bride worthy of becoming a Fairweather wife, Stephen Fairweather had done so without much of a fight. But in a move no one expected, he made Bonnie a permanent fixture in their lives, requiring her to work as his new wife's companion forevermore.

"But there will be no land or any future if John Richards is not swayed to marry you, Willa," Bonnie intoned, cutting her meat carefully as any grand lady would. "Invite him for another visit now that the repairs are done on the bridge."

Knowing not to argue, Willa nodded. "I will."

"And do not allow your time with Richards to conflict with those visits from Dr. Anderson." Bonnie paused in her cutting, issuing a clear message with her stern gaze. "Sharing is not something men handle very well."

Not caring to be chastised as if she were a child, Willa's temper roared to life, burning as hot as the flames in the dining room's ornate fireplace. "And yet, some women are required to do so for a lifetime."

She should not have said it.

It was reckless.

It was dangerous.

It would get them all in trouble.

Her statement elicited a gasp from Lucy and a horrified look from her mother. Bonnie remained unmoved, as did Cal when their father laid his knife and fork down to address her.

"I've never been the type of man to turn away a free service." He didn't raise his voice—he never did—that deadly calm her father possessed was enough to frighten anyone. "But I will end Dr. Anderson's time at Haven House if he hinders an attachment between you and Richards. I'll even go as far as to suggest to Ulrich that he send his nephew away. Is that what you want, Wilhelmina?"

"No, sir." Head down, Willa searched for a reason to let Noah continue his visits. "I believe we're making progress, and Dr. Anderson's treatments are helping me become stronger so I can be a good wife to John Richards."

None of that was true. While she and Noah did use their time to discuss her health, they also spent entirely too much time chatting about other things. Bonnie knew this as the eyes and ears of the house, yet she remained surprisingly silent.

"That's good to hear," her father said, and with that, rose from the table and left them.

Having gone pale there at the end, Cal went for his wine glass when the dining room door clicked closed, and their father was well and truly gone. "Thank you, Bonnie."

Bonnie didn't reply, too busy assessing Margaret. "How are you doing down there?"

Willa noticed her mother appeared more angry than scared now that they were alone. "Thank you for alerting us to his arrival," her mother said to Bonnie. "I knew we were close to the mill's holiday closing date, but I didn't think it would be this soon."

"The mill is slowing down for the holidays earlier than normal because of the lack of pine harvest. That means he'll be home from here until January arrives." Bonnie took a deep draw from her own wine goblet. "Everyone best ready themselves."

"I'll write to John this afternoon while you visit with Noah," Lucy said, her voice barely above a whisper. "We should know by tomorrow when he's available to visit."

"Why are *you* writing to him, Lucy?" Cal asked.

Lucy's smile brightened in an instant. "John and I are friends, much like Dr. Anderson and Willa."

Margaret paused in bringing her wine goblet to her lips, staring at Willa over its rim. In the last couple of years, her mother had become many things.

Evil.

Spiteful.

Hateful in a way no one outside their family would ever truly be able to comprehend.

But Margaret was also cunning to a fault. Her intellect was the single gift she had bestowed upon Willa. Grace had received her beauty, and Lucy had gained her ability to easily manage social situations, but when it came to herself, Willa knew her keenness for knowledge came solely from their mother.

"This is your one and only warning," Margaret said. "Do you understand, Wilhelmina?"

"Yes, mother."

CHAPTER 8

The afternoon rain arrived earlier than normal. It was the proper three o'clock downpour, only today, it swept in an hour early. So, when the allotted time for Noah's arrival came and went, Willa assumed the weather had kept him away, and she decided to do what she did best.

Hide in the conservatory.

With a book in her lap and a few cats curled atop her as she snuggled under her favorite blanket, Willa spent an hour reading before deciding to stop and tackle Dickens. Christmas would be here before they realized and she needed to be prepared.

Not that she hadn't read the novel at least two dozen times.

Flipping through the pages, she searched for a good place to start, never caring for the beginning of the novel. Why Mr. Dickens insisted on starting so many of his tales in such a depressing way was beyond her. There was enough of that nonsense in the real world.

No, she much more enjoyed something spectacular. If there were to be elements of gloom and despair in her stories, then she wanted tales with a proper monster to root for or even a villain who was so intriguing that it left her debating on who should win in the end.

"What's this?" she murmured when a neatly folded piece of paper dropped into her lap. Setting the book aside, she opened it and grinned at her own messy handwriting.

A Christmas Promise
by: Wilhelmina Fairweather (age 10)

Instead of using her usual library copy of *A Christmas Carol*, Willa had chosen to be lazy and simply grabbed the old edition she kept here in the conservatory. The poor thing obviously hadn't been opened in quite a few years, and as she read the poem, the memory of writing it had her smile growing even wider.

On Christmas Eve night
three little children lay in bed
whispering to the fourth
who should be dead

I will always love you
said the oldest and most fair
She was lovely and kind
without a worry to spare

And I will always be your friend
said the youngest and most brave
for there was never a moment
where her courage might cave

The one who should be dead
thanked them both sincerely
she hugged her sisters close
knowing they loved her dearly

But the final one
their brother most severe
handsome and charming
never having a fear

He spoke soft and swift
in the deep, dark night
I will care for you always
but we will have to fight

Whatever do you mean
asked his sisters with concern
for they knew all too well
how his darkness could churn

Tie up loose ends
that's what we must do
for once that is done,
we can take care of you

And so, on that Christmas Eve night
the Fairweather children huddled in tight
making oaths and promises to each other
speaking things best not heard by their father or mother

They would stay the course
and escape somehow
perhaps one day
if the fates allow

Goodness, that was atrocious. However, the day it was written had
been a special one where Willa finally understood how much her siblings
loved her. The four of them had snuggled together on her bed, making

grandiose plans for the future as she recovered from an attack. Cal had been so serious about it all, ready to do whatever he needed to get her help. Some of the ideas he had put forth were quite terrifying, but back then he was known to occasionally use the most dastardly methods to gain what he wanted.

Thankfully, he eventually grew out of that phase; otherwise, who knows what type of man he would have become.

Tucking the paper back into the book, Willa settled on her lounger and began to read. However, somewhere around Ebenezer's visit from the Ghost of Christmas Present, Willa's eyes grew heavy. Not sleeping well had become a theme in her life. Between the occasional singing which continued to plague her nights, albeit much less now, and her quite improper dreams of Noah, she was hardly getting any rest.

And she must have dozed off because the next thing Willa knew, she was in yet another dream with Noah. This time, they were in the forest. Hidden from the world like the mill worker and his sweetheart. With her back against an old oak tree, Noah's lips ravaged hers while his hand made its way up her skirt.

It had been deliciously wicked, not at all proper, and absolutely everything Willa wanted to experience. But she wanted more—so much more.

She just wasn't sure *what exactly.*

The heavy ache that always followed these Noah-filled dreams settled in her bones. Crawling around in the very marrow, making demands that she could never fulfill.

The dream over, Willa stretched with a wide yawn. Her waking consciousness slowly rose to greet life again, and as it did, a keen sense of being watched sent a warning down her spine.

Popping one eye open, a second quickly followed, both taking in the sight of Noah sitting directly across from her in the only other chair on the lower level. He wore his usual white shirt, his suspenders showing since he must have left his jacket somewhere. The dark wool pants he wore were blotchy from the rain, while his hair was more than a little soaked and brushed back from those hypnotic blue eyes with which he studied her. Behind him, the pitter-patter of rain against the glass wall had lessened substantially compared to when she first settled down to read.

"You look quite peaceful when you sleep."

Lifting herself into a sitting position, Willa patted the bun atop her head to ensure it had remained properly intact. It had, but at the first touch, the shell black rubber comb came loose, and her hair fell in a cascade across her shoulders. The small smile on Noah's lips faltered, and she blushed—truly blushed—thinking she must look a sight.

"My apologies," Noah murmured. "I didn't mean to startle you."

Willa swung her legs to the side of the chaise lounge, unsettling the cats and accidentally knocking her book onto the brick floor. She and Noah swept down simultaneously to pick up the tome, nearly colliding with one another in the process.

And with him crouched low and her barely hanging off the settee, they froze, each with a hand on the book.

"I want you to walk with me," Noah whispered, his throat bobbing as he worked through whatever was going on in his head. "When the rain stops."

"You know my lungs don't do well in moist air," she whispered in return. "I can't go out in the rain."

Noah released his grip on the book, but not before his index finger slid delicately down hers. The touch was simple, an accident perhaps, but that didn't stop the rush of its effects on her body. Suddenly, she was back in the forest of her dreams, allowing this man to have her however he wanted.

"What did I tell you at The Gathering?" His whispering deepened to an almost sinful level, and Willa fought a sigh. She was getting to be as bad as Lucy. "With me, you can do anything. I'll never allow you to come to harm and will always judge every situation accordingly. You're what's important, Willa."

Willa snapped up to sitting, almost smacking Noah's perfectly proportioned face with her forehead. "Th-the rain will probably fa-all until dusk."

Was she stuttering?

"A-and I can't go out at night." She *was* stuttering, and for some reason, her mouth thought it a good idea to continue talking. "We can go another day."

"Why can't you go out at night?"

She really had no idea. Alone in the dark with Noah sounded like a perfectly solid plan. "My mother."

The threat of Margaret Fairweather would have been enough to give any sane man pause, but too bad for her, Noah Anderson decided to prove he was indeed not sane.

"You're a grown woman." He straightened to settle back in his chair. "Besides, I need to speak with you in private."

"About?"

"Private things." He studied her for a moment. "This house has ears, and I do not wish for what I have to say to be known."

Willa didn't need to turn and look. The warning was there. Bonnie must be lingering in the doorway.

"It could take hours for the rain to stop."

He gave an arrogant shrug. "It won't."

And it would seem that even God Almighty wasn't immune to Noah Anderson's charm. Not but a second passed, and the storm abruptly ended. There was no tapering off, just a complete halt as if commanded.

Noah stood and held out his hand. "Shall we?"

Willa gasped as the horse turned unexpectedly.

"You have ridden on a horse before, haven't you?"

Keenly aware of every muscle in his thighs cradling her from behind, Willa nodded from her spot on the saddle. She hoped she wasn't holding the horse's mane too tight. The animal didn't seem to mind, but it couldn't exactly tell her if her grip was causing it pain.

"Relax, Willa," Noah said directly in her ear, and her eyes went wide. He was so close. "I want you to focus on your breathing. We're not going far. Just to the beach."

Focus on her breathing? Impossible. She could only focus on the brush of his lips against her ear.

"Why the beach?"

"Because you said you wanted to visit it."

"And?" Twisting in the saddle, she looked over her shoulder at him. "There must be another reason."

"There isn't. Whatever Wilhelmina Fairweather wants, she will always get if I have a say in it." Noah guided the horse down the clay lane, leaving Haven House in the dust behind them. "Hold on tight. I'm going to let her run. If you need me to stop or slow down, just tap my leg."

"Wait, what?"

Tangling her fingers in the horse's mane, Willa squealed as the beast shot into a run with only a click of Noah's tongue. Whenever she went into town with her family, they took a carriage, and with her body unfamiliar with how to handle the ride, she bounced in the saddle.

The stiffness in her muscles didn't help, and knowing she would be sore tomorrow, Willa attempted to calm the strain, allowing the beauty of the moment to sink in.

And it really was a beautiful moment.

As the forest rushed past and the steady beat of hooves thundered under her, Willa began to feel giddy and lighthearted, almost like a child. Noah hadn't given her any time to fix her hair, and she'd been forced to leave it loose, the wind knocking it about wildly.

She was still grinning like a loon when they reached the end of the lane before the horse crossed the road that traveled between Hollingsdale and Port Michaelson. With a quick tug on the reins, Noah guided them straight onto a narrow path where the brush hugged the edges. Branches and shrubbery caught on to her skirt before breaking, and realizing she had arched forward as if she were some jockey in a race, Willa leaned back slightly.

"Almost there." Noah's arm snaked around her waist, anchoring her against his chest. "We should make it in time to see the sunset."

Beneath them, the clay gave way to a muddy brown and then to the granules of packed dirt that she hadn't seen in ages. The path ahead curved, and as they made the bend, the beach appeared—an empty, wild expanse of color. The powder white sand, the blue and greens of the water, and a sky filled with various shades of pink and purple made for a spectacular sight.

Noah clicked his tongue again, and the horse switched from a light canter into a full gallop. Barreling to the water's edge, it turned at the very last minute, running along the line of crashing waves. The spray of the salty air chased them, and Willa found herself laughing with excitement.

"I've got you." Noah's hold tightened. "Put your arms out and fly, Willa."

She didn't have to be told twice and held her arms out as they sped down the length of the beach. Free. This is what it felt like to be free. There were no worries about her breathing. No worries about her father. No John Richards. No uncertain future.

There was only Noah.

Steady and strong, and allowing her to spread her wings.

The ride continued until they reached a section of the beach met by the forest. He slowed their pace, instructing the horse to walk instead of run.

"How was that?"

"Marvelous!" Willa bent forward to hug the horse's neck. "You are now my dearest friend, and I don't even know your name."

"Her name is Hope."

Willa laughed. Irony was a staple in her life, and sometimes, it was best just to accept it. "Well, we are now friends for life, Hope."

She patted the smooth brown of Hope's coat and didn't miss Noah clearing his throat. "I feel as though Hope's handler deserves that same affirmation of friendship."

"Does he?" Willa returned to sitting upright, refusing to acknowledge that his arm remained firmly around her waist. Or how wonderful it felt to have it there. "Perhaps."

"He most certainly does." With a tight pull on the reins, Noah brought Hope to a stop and swung down. "Let's walk."

He helped her dismount. It was not a graceful endeavor, but he was kind enough not to laugh, even when she nearly toppled directly over his head.

Holding her at the waist, he bit down a grin as she settled on solid ground. "Are you sure you've ridden a horse?"

"Of course I have. I've just never ridden astride." Willa held her head high, and Hope had the decency to snort on her behalf. "See, Hope believes me."

"Women always stick together." He smiled, devastating her as he seemed born to do. "It's the law of the universe."

As with any time after a storm, the waves roared, and gusts of wind sped about in every direction. Willa's unbound hair smacked across her face, and she tried not to choke as the strands gagged her.

"What did you wish to talk to me about?"

The question caused the mischievous glint in Noah's eyes to shift, dulling them to an alarming degree.

"Your sister."

A coward at her core, Willa couldn't meet his gaze. "What did they tell you about Grace?" she asked, staring at the water. "Whatever it is, I can explain."

"Er, no." Placing two fingers under her chin, Noah forced her to look at him. "I mean, yes, my aunt did tell me about Grace, but you'll never have to explain her reasons. I can understand completely why she did what she did."

Willa's brows snapped together. There was no telling what wild story his aunt had spouted off or what other rumor was being perpetrated by her own family. "What exactly do you think Grace did?"

"She fell in love."

He stepped forward, leaving an inappropriate amount of space between them—one, maybe two inches. If either were to take a large inhale, their chests would touch, and that thought alone overrode her concerns of him knowing about Grace.

"Falling in love with someone who your parents don't approve of isn't a crime, Willa."

It was if you were a Fairweather.

"He was a mill worker," she said, her voice nearly drowning in the sea of noise surrounding them. "His name was Tommy, and he had a dog—a big Dane almost as tall as Grace. She loved dogs, you see, and when she happened upon Tommy and his dog walking through the forest on their way to work his shift at the mill, she couldn't help but stop him to meet the animal."

It hurt. It had been two years, and it still hurt. To lose Grace... She would carry that pain forever.

"When Tommy saw her, he was a goner, and to be fair, no man who ever laid eyes on our Grace managed to walk away without being a little in love. She was special. I would say beautiful, but the word is so inadequate." Willa's lips twisted into a wry grin. "She looked very much like my mother."

Noah made a face of disgust before catching himself. "Apologies, but your mother is not what I envision when you say the word beautiful."

Willa openly cackled. It did seem a bit preposterous. "My mother was quite the beauty before my father made her into what she is today."

"Well, she does frown more than most, and I guess all that frowning has caused her to..." He trailed off, pressing his lips together. "I'm sorry."

"Don't be. The only reason I know Grace resembled what our mother once looked like is because of the honeymoon portrait hanging in the upstairs hallway. My father commissioned it after their wedding."

It was always hard for visitors to tell whether the painting was of Margaret or Grace, which is why the portrait was moved upstairs. With golden hair and bewitching hazel eyes, their mother had once been a great prize to be won. But where her smile sat tightly on her lips, guarded and reserved, Grace's smile was never such a way. Warm with an absolute wholesomeness shining through, Grace's entire soul could be seen in her smile.

"But where my mother is short, Grace is tall like me," Willa continued. "It's one of the few physical traits we shared. Well, that and our freckles. She and I have the same matching pattern on our wrists."

Noah's warm hand came around to rest on her lower back, and she went rigid before realizing he was turning her to walk along the shore with him. Hope trailed behind, apparently not needing to be told to follow.

"You and Grace don't look alike? But you said she was beautiful."

The cool air circled them as they walked, but she didn't mind. While Noah hadn't given her time to fix her hair, he had made sure she was bundled properly in a coat. The dampness she expected was a mere afterthought, even with winter's fingers digging their way in for the season.

"No, we're not alike at all. Grace was perfect in every way." Her sister's face filled her mind, making Willa's head hurt. "Well, not completely perfect. She had a scar under her right eye that I unfortunately gave her. On one of those rare, good days I had as a child, Bonnie took us outside to fly kites. I didn't know what to do and was so excited that I mistakenly allowed my string to become wrapped around Grace's head as we played. It eventually got so tight the string sliced her cheek, leaving a scar. My mother said I was lucky I hadn't taken out her eye, and I was inconsolable for weeks in my guilt."

"Was Grace upset?"

"Grace never got upset about anything and would say the scar served as a reminder of when her little sister was able to come outside and play."

Noah's hand dropped from her lower back, and Willa didn't want its loss to bother her so, but it did. She nearly stopped and demanded he return it.

"I know Grace ran off with Tommy, and your parents forbid her from returning to Haven House, but you'll see her again one day." He glanced ahead at the rise of sand pines in the distance. The thick cluster served as the barrier between the wild forest and the beach. "I bet every time she looks in the mirror and sees her scar, she thinks of you."

Willa schooled her features, wishing that could be true. "Why did you want to talk about Grace?"

He winced. Not much, but enough to set her on edge. "I didn't. I wanted to talk about Lucy."

CHAPTER 9

S he did stop walking then, giving him her full attention. "What about Lucy?"

Noah's unwavering gaze met her own. "Paul isn't going to propose."

"What?" Her shout echoed around the dunes, the sea oats atop them waving in a frenzy as the wind picked up speed. "Why ever not?"

Rubbing the back of his neck, he hesitated, but Hope would have none of that and nudged him with her snout. "Paul wants to marry someone else, and I'm telling you this to soften the blow for her, Willa. Ulrich plans to visit Haven House next week to deal with the news."

She spun away from him, pacing on the sand. "But there is an agreement!"

"No, there was an assumption," he corrected gently. "On your father's part."

"Don't patronize me." Hands fisted at her side, she yelled louder, utterly outraged on her sister's behalf. "Paul Anderson would be lucky to have Lucy. How could he possibly object?"

Noah followed her. "Willa, watch your breathing."

"Stop reminding me to breathe!" she screamed, chest pumping and eyes wild. "You will not tell me my sister's one hope in life—her one dream—will be ruined because Paul Anderson doesn't think she's worthy enough to be his wife."

He was in front of her in a heartbeat, grasping her by the upper arms. "I never said he didn't think she was worthy. Lucy is a lovely girl, and Paul is an idiot. My uncle nearly killed him when he said he wanted to marry someone else."

Willa sobered immediately. "What?"

"A young woman who came to The Gathering caught his eye, and they've been meeting secretly. It's an entire group that gathers on the far end of this very beach, right where the bayou joins the sea."

She stared at him as if he were insane. There had been plenty of women at The Gathering, but Paul didn't show any of them attention except... "One of the serving girls from Port Michaelson?"

Slowly, he nodded. "Her name is Katie, and Ulrich wasn't happy, but his own marriage was a love match, so he can't fault his son for following his heart."

Could anyone fault another person for following their heart? The answer was no, but at the moment, Willa's single concern lay with her sister.

"My father..." Air wheezed past her lips, and she pressed a hand to her stomach. This wasn't a breathing attack but pure terror manifesting itself. "He'll blame Lucy."

"But it's not Lucy's fault."

"He won't care!"

She couldn't stand still and continued to march as fast as she could along the sandy shore. There was no destination in mind, only a burst of energy propelling her into motion.

"Lucy will find someone else." Noah chased after her, as did Hope. "I didn't lie when I said she was lovely. Lucy will make a fine wife to any man."

"What man?" Willa halted, spreading her arms wide at the empty landscape. "What man, Noah? We're in the middle of nowhere. Hollingsdale isn't exactly a bustling city filled with available suitors, and

Port Michaelson is worse. It's nothing but dock workers and brothels. Where is she to find a gentleman among them?"

"Grace found love with a mill worker." His own anger was close to the surface, and the muscle in Noah's jaw ticked ominously. "Why can't Lucy do the same? Why does it have to be some gentleman?"

It was as if he had struck her. Noah couldn't possibly understand. He couldn't possibly know what he was suggesting.

"Because there is no other choice." She would not cry. Not in this beautiful place. Not with him watching. She had been broken a thousand times—in a thousand ways—but she would not permit it to happen now. "Lucy is to go to Paul Anderson so the mills can unite. I am to go to John Richards so the mills can use his land for future growth. There is no other option. Fairweather Lumber and the Anderson Mill cannot survive without them being united."

He was in her space again, crowding her as the sun began to set behind him. On any other day, she would have marveled at the magnificent show playing out, but in the here and now, with the world crashing down on her, Willa didn't care. Too lost in her anger and the pain she saw flashing in Noah's eyes, her stomach turned completely over at his next words.

"Paul and Katie want to marry at Christmas. Ulrich has already approached your brother and asked him to announce the news to your father."

"My brother?"

"I told you, a group of them meet. The girls from Port Michaelson, Paul, your brother, my brother, and... me."

She had no right to want to claw his eyes out. He was her doctor. She was his patient. There was nothing else to it. No matter their long talks in the library. No matter that she had opened up to him more than anyone.

"I see."

The evil man grinned. "Oh, do you?"

"I do."

"No, I don't think you do."

Crossing her arms, she refused to allow the quick prick of jealousy to rule and kept her voice even. "Where do you meet? In your little 'medical' cottage?"

Both she and Lucy had seen the place. It was surprisingly stocked, outfitted with equipment sent by Noah's friends from up north.

His infuriating grin deepened. "If I didn't know any better, I would think you were jealous, Wilhelmina Fairweather."

"I don't know what you mean."

Noah was completely upon her. Swooping in to wrap an arm around her waist, their bodies collided together. "Yes, you do."

"This is my brother's doing," she said, her body warring over whether she should try to wiggle free from his hold or stay put. "Cal and father have been arguing endlessly over Cal's wild idea to end the mill and focus more on something called land development."

"It's a sound plan," Noah replied, having the audacity to agree. "Advancements in lumber processing are happening far faster than the Anderson or the Fairweather mills can keep up with. The end is near, Willa. Ulrich already agrees it's best to sell once Paul takes over their company in a few years. He's begun looking into other ventures that will work best for our family, just as Cal has been trying to do with your father."

"But if the mills unite and I go to Richards, both families can survive." She pounded his chest with her fist. One good solid strike to make herself feel better. "We can make it work."

He took her beating, almost looking happy to do it. "But for how long? It's no longer possible to go on for endless decades like they've done before. The world is changing, Willa. Every corner of it."

And she would have no idea. Tucked away at Haven House, she would have no idea what changes were occurring in the world or what new possibilities were on the horizon.

"I'm going to murder Cal." She shoved Noah away so she could continue her march onward. "He's been away all afternoon, but he's here, isn't he? He's meeting with your women!"

"They're not my women, Willa," he called after her, his denial only enraging her further. "I leave before things turn...well—before things begin."

That had her stopping. "What things?"

"Things I'm not about to explain."

Willa's eyes narrowed into slits, mainly because of the sand blowing about in the wind, but she measured the look with just enough distaste that she hoped it made him think it was because of his reply.

"It's Jennie." She wrinkled her nose. "The one with the freckles and the ample bosom. That's the one you like."

Noah tipped his head back and said something to the sky before giving her his attention once again. "No, I don't like her."

"Why not?" she asked, seemingly upset on Jennie's behalf, even though if Noah did find her attractive, she would hate the woman for life. "She's stunning and seems to be lovely."

"She is lovely," he said as he edged closer. "And kind and clever and well-read."

Well, there it was. Willa had never had a mortal enemy before, but she had always wanted one. A real Caroline Bingley to her Lizzie Bennett, and it would seem Jennie fit the bill. Lovely, kind, clever, and well-read Jennie.

"How wonderful for her," she replied, pure acid dripping from every syllable. "It must be exhausting to be so very accomplished."

Noah barked out a laugh, the sound competing with the roar of the waves. "I would imagine so, especially when using those accomplishments to make Cal fall in love with her."

Her mouth dropped open. Cal? No. He wouldn't dare. He knew his place. He understood the requirements of being an heir and would never jeopardize his position. "That's not possible."

"Perhaps he and Paul can have a double ceremony after the holidays."

He was joking, but this wasn't a joke. Her father...her father would murder Cal if he got wind of this. Women were nothing to her brother, and while he would eventually settle down when required, it would never be with someone like Jennie.

"Where is Cal?" Already hurrying ahead, she vaguely knew of the place Noah referred to as their meeting spot. When she and her siblings were children, their mother occasionally brought them to the beach to walk among the dunes. Willa had only been able to accompany the family twice, but she remembered every detail. "I must speak with him right away."

CHAPTER 10

"Willa, you need to calm down."

"A word of advice, Dr. Anderson." Rounding on him as she reached the line in the sand where the forest met the beach, Willa pointed a finger in Noah's face. "The very last thing you should ever tell a Fairweather woman to do is calm down."

He held his hands in the air, his smirk firmly in place. "Understood."

She shot forward again, finding a small, worn path through the trees. However, she didn't get far before Noah grabbed her by the arm. "I said no, Willa. Things are happening over there that are not for you to see."

"Then why did you bring me here?"

"Because I wanted to make you happy and have one of those desires of yours come true," he said plainly. "I also wanted to talk without Bonnie attempting to listen in on our conversation. She certainly is a busybody when it comes to you. It's almost like she's part of the family and not a staff member."

Bonnie.

The perfect story to make him understand how badly her father would take the news of Paul and this Katie girl.

"She is a member of the family, except not by blood. My father is in love with Bonnie. He has been ever since he was a boy."

It was incredibly satisfying to see Noah's mouth fall open, and she patiently waited while he wrapped his mind around the whole thing.

"I...um...didn't know."

"Why should you?" Willa shrugged her shoulders. "It's not as if we air the information for all to know."

He truly was struggling. Noah was a brilliant man but also a good one. Grasping how devious the Fairweathers could be wasn't something people like him were forced to do very often. "So, your mother allows your father's mistress to serve on the household staff?"

She would have found his reasoning funny if the situation were not so serious. "Bonnie is not my father's mistress. She is as chaste as the day she was born. At least, I hope she is."

"Then why—"

"My father hired Bonnie when he married my mother, and she accepted because she wanted to be close to him."

"But what were his reasons for offering her the job in the first place if not to keep her as a mistress?" The cruelty behind it was finally settling over him. "Wouldn't that just be torture for them both?"

"The long and the short of it is that Stephen Fairweather doesn't like other people touching his things. In his mind, Bonnie is his possession, and he keeps her close so she can never be with another man. He loves her in his strange, twisted way, but his dedication to duty overrides that love. He married my mother to keep the mill going. Her dowry was exactly what he needed, so he gave up his Bonnie for stability."

Noah let out a heavy sigh as it all came crashing down on him. Resting a shoulder against a tree trunk, he stared at her. "Which is why you think he'll not accept this whole situation with Paul and Lucy."

"He'll think that if he had to sacrifice the love of his life, then why shouldn't others do the same. It will send him into a rage, Noah. He'll blame Lucy. I know he will. He'll say she didn't do enough to encourage a courtship between herself and Paul." Willa slouched against her own tree trunk. "And with Cal and Jennie, it'll be much worse. So much worse."

"Perhaps I can speak with him."

Willa opened her mouth to tell him that was the worst idea possible, but before she could do so, a faint singing carried through the trees. Above them, the branches rustled in the wind, drowning out the haunting song for a moment or two.

But then it came again.

"Do you hear that?"

Noah frowned. "Hear what?"

"The song." She held up her hand, silencing his reply. "Can you hear the song?"

Grace's song—the same song she had been hearing during the night—was coming from somewhere deep in the heart of the forest, and Willa strained to listen. It was most definitely her sister's singing.

As if in a trance, she began to walk into the darkening wood. Twilight would be upon them soon, and once it covered the land, they would have a hard time finding their way back to Hope without a lantern.

But Willa couldn't think about that. She had to discover the source of the singing. Who was out there tormenting her? Who was breaking her heart all over again?

Noah was not as interested. "It's time to go back." He caught up and laid his hands gently on her shoulders. "It was wrong to bring you here."

On a mission, she shrugged off his hold on her. "I want to see who is singing."

Not knowing exactly what to expect when they departed Haven House, she had thankfully donned her walking boots, making her hurried trek through the forest easy.

"We're close to where they meet." Noah moved to stand in front of her, his large body completely blocking the way. "What you're hearing is probably Melinda. She likes to sing for us."

A raging heat erupted in the center of her body, exploding like a fiery pulse through every fiber of her being. With it, a bloody haze dragged across her vision, its tendrils curling around Noah's beautiful face. "Sing for you?" she said, only slightly concerned by the screeching pitch her tone had taken. "These gatherings sound like a rather fun time. Too bad you never invited me. I've been told I sing quite well."

A lie.

She couldn't sing.

Bonnie's cats carried a tune better than she did.

"Oh, so you sing?" he asked, approaching her as if she were a wild animal who might startle easily. "Is there anything you can't do, Ms. Fairweather?"

"Do not tease."

"Oh, but I so enjoy it." He lifted a hand hesitantly, his fingers tucking a strand of hair behind her ear. "That look that enters your eyes whenever you're pretending to be upset over something I've said is incredible. It makes me crave things I shouldn't, but I can't help it. I want you glaring daggers at me all the time."

"Ah, I see. You're a masochist." She would not smile, fighting its emergence to the bitter end. "I cannot say I'm surprised."

"Why is that?" The hand in her hair coasted lower, skating along her jaw to cradle it. "Because I'm a doctor?"

"Of course. Your kind likes to learn through pain."

His thumb stroked her cheek while she bravely held his stare. The last time they had been this close was when she tripped on the path to his medical cottage weeks ago. Only this time, there was no Lucy or John Richards waiting around the bend. This time, it was just the two of them, their breath mingling together in the cool winter air.

"I have not touched those women, Willa."

"And I do not care."

The serious expression that had taken over him suddenly transformed back into the arrogant smirk he carried around so effortlessly.

"Liar."

"I am not," she said, more to the tree she was staring at than him. "And I'm quite offended that you would call me such."

"There are several things I'm going to say that might offend you," he countered. "Things you won't mind hearing. Things you'll be begging me to say and perhaps begging me to do."

A crimson hue proceeded to cover every inch of skin on her entire body. She was naïve to such things but understood the undercurrent of what he was implying.

Around them, the singing changed, going from Grace's light, ethereal tones to something deeper and more robust. It mixed with a giggling like the night she first heard it.

This time, Noah heard it, too. "Is that the song?"

"Yes, and the person who has been singing at night." She listened a little longer. "I recognize the giggling."

"That's Jennie." Noah dropped his hand from her face. "It's time for us to go."

The singing stopped, turning into a muffled conversation. They must not be far off, and Willa was determined. "Not until I speak with my brother."

She followed the sound, with Noah hissing after her to stop. A break in the trees and brush was up ahead, and the sounds of water rushing past overtook the voices. Their words were hardly discernible now, coming across more like grunts.

Not far behind, Noah seized her arm just as Willa broke partly through the bushes and came to an abrupt stop right on the edge of the brown, murky river of water flowing past. It had always been strange to Willa how the blue of fresh water and the turquoise of the sea could merge to make such a disgusting shade of brown. Brackish is what they called it, and the muddy color filled the numerous dune lakes and small rivers connecting the bayous with the ocean.

But Willa wasn't looking at the water.

She was staring at the opposite shore

And directly at a naked Paul Anderson moving between a woman's legs.

The distance between them wasn't all that great, with the river of brackish sludge no more than perhaps twelve feet across. She was quite certain she remained hidden, partially obscured by the trees and bushes lining the shore.

Not that either Paul or the woman would notice anything. A dragon could swoop down to obliterate them both with a single breath, and the pair wouldn't even acknowledge its presence.

"Goodness," she exhaled, hypnotized by Paul rutting wildly between the woman's thighs. The couple was on a blanket, the woman crying out in abandon with every strike. "*Goodness.*"

Noah stood at her back, his hand sliding forward to rest on her stomach. "Come along, Willa," he whispered in her ear. "This is not for us to see."

She ignored his command. "Do men always do that during the act?"

"Do what?"

"Flop around in such a way?" she asked. "It looks rather animalistic."

Noah's chuckle had her shivering. "Give Paul the benefit of the doubt here. He's excited and attempting to find his rhythm." The hand on her stomach moved higher, stopping at her ribs. "But to answer your question, yes. When it's good between a man and a woman, they can lose themselves to their animalistic natures."

Katie cried out, and the sound echoed through the trees. Willa's eyes went wide. "Is he hurting her?"

"No."

The echoed cries shifted to moans, and combined with the slap of flesh and the sight of Paul's muscular ass straining as he moved faster, Willa's curiosity only grew. "Then why is she making those noises?"

Noah's hand pressed against her ribs, his thumb stroking her lower breast. Unlike their first meeting, the move this time was completely intentional, and she shouldn't allow it.

But she did and even arched for more.

"We can discuss this on the way back to Haven."

"No, I will hear it now."

Noah's lips grazed her ear as he spoke. "Because Katie likes feeling Paul buried deep inside her."

"That's very hard to believe."

In an obviously well-practiced move, Katie flipped Paul to his back, and the remnants of the chemise she wore were shucked over her head to be tossed on the sand.

"What is she... *oh my.*"

If Willa thought she couldn't peel her eyes away before, she was mistaken. Totally enthralled, she stared at a naked Katie riding Paul as if she were riding a wild stallion. A blur of motion, the sight could almost be considered beautiful if one took the time to think about it. With her head thrown back and her large breasts swaying as Paul's hands gripped her hips to encourage her on, Katie looked rather magnificent as she took control.

And when Paul lifted his head to speak softly to her, Willa found herself leaning forward to listen.

"Paul is telling her how good she's doing." Noah's thumb continued to stroke her breast, the light touch causing goosebumps to explode across her skin. "And how much he likes the way she takes him into her body."

"Oh."

The couple's screams grew, punctuated by Paul hammering into Katie from below. Holding her above him, his thick cock worked in and out, slamming upward at a speed that had Willa biting her bottom lip.

"That's awfully fast."

Noah's forehead dropped to her shoulder as if he couldn't continue to watch. His breathing had turned heavy, and Willa's hand curled at her side. She desperately wanted to reach behind her and touch him. To know if what they were seeing was affecting him as much as it was her.

"Paul is close," he whispered.

"Close to what?"

Noah didn't need to answer because just then Paul *shattered*.

There was no other word for it. Mouth open and face twisted into a snarl, Paul shouted as he worked Katie brutally up and down his cock. He drove into her without mercy, filling the woman completely until he shook like a leaf trembling in the wind.

Too lost in what she was seeing, Willa didn't notice her brother exit the woods with Jennie on his arm until Cal's laughter attracted her attention. He was saying something to Jennie, and whatever it was had her dropping to her knees and ripping at the ties on his trousers.

Willa turned away with a gasp. She pushed past Noah and found the trail again, walking towards the beach with every bit of her skin aflame with a needy desire she couldn't put into words.

Noah kept his distance, giving her time to think. She was so very thankful for that because if she were honest, she wouldn't know what to do or say to him if he hadn't.

Hope was waiting, the sky above now a deep shade of blue since the sun had already said its goodbye to the world. Going straight to the horse, Willa vigorously petted the animal's snout, the emotions and sensations running through her needing an outlet.

Questions.

She had so many questions.

Was what she just witnessed normal? Would John Richards do those things to her? Would she do what Katie was doing to John Richards? Would it hurt? How did it work?

"Why do they always get on their knees?"

Her insatiable curiosity had the question slipping off her tongue. The mill worker's sweetheart and Jennie had both fallen to their knees in the same manner, and Willa didn't understand why.

Sensing Noah approaching from the forest, she kept her focus on Hope. "I once happened upon a mill worker who was meeting his woman in the forest. She got on her knees just as Jennie did a moment ago, and I have yet to figure out what they were doing."

"Willa, look at me."

His gruff tone was infused with whatever emotion was running through her bloodstream. That hidden primal part of her body recognized it immediately, pulling at something in her lower stomach and down to the throbbing pulse between her legs.

"Please answer my question." She could not possibly look at him. "You're my doctor and should be able to explain."

"I'm also a man."

"Pretend you're not."

His laughter shot out across the beach, startling both Willa and the horse. "After watching Paul in all his glory while holding you... that's very much impossible."

"Please try." Willa glanced at him over her shoulder, somewhat shocked by the intensity staring back at her. He looked like a wire strung tight and ready to snap. "For me, Noah."

Hearing his name on her lips had his eyes shuttering. "She was going to take him into her mouth."

"But why?"

He muttered something to himself, almost sounding like he was asking God for strength. "Because the tight, wetness of the mouth simulates the feeling of being inside a woman."

Hope grunted in appreciation as Willa spun around to give Noah her full attention, completely fascinated. "*Really?*"

"Yes," he grated out, the tick in his jaw returning. "If done correctly."

"But can't a woman become pregnant doing this?"

"No."

Concerned he would break his jaw due to how tightly he was clenching it, Willa shrugged. "Then what is the point?"

"Pleasure."

She frowned, her brows drawing tight. "I cannot imagine it being pleasurable to have a man ramming himself into my mouth such as Paul was doing between poor Katie's legs. One might lose a tooth if the person thrusting were unable to control himself."

Eyes bulging in disbelief, Noah let out a strangled sound. "Some women enjoy it. Some women do not," he replied. "But all women enjoy it being done to them."

Willa's mouth formed a perfect O. Whatever did he mean?

"Explain."

Noah lifted his face to the heavens, talking to God again.

"Noah Anderson, you are a doctor, so act like a doctor," she huffed, the fear of him thinking her an idiot making her snappish. "Explain it to me as if you were speaking to a colleague."

Another strangled laugh. "You are not my colleague, Willa. You are—"

"Yes, yes, I know. Your patient."

"—the woman I want above all others." His head dropped, the last of the day's sunlight highlighting his beauty. "And I would use my tongue, Willa. I would bury my face between your legs for hours, feasting on you until the only word left in your vocabulary is my name. *My name.* I will have you screaming it, demanding more."

"More of what?" She was so very frustrated and couldn't believe what she was hearing. "Tell me, please."

"Tell you?" He stalked towards her. "I would rather show you."

Hope snorted at his forwardness.

Willa gaped at him in shock.

And the wintery wind halted around them, allowing what Noah said next to be heard loud and clear.

"One word from you, Willa." His arm dipped around her waist, drawing their bodies together until something like a *guh* came out of her. "One word is all the permission I need to drop to my knees, lift your skirts, and have you riding my tongue until you're coming apart."

CHAPTER 11

"**G**oing once."

Willa's brain alerted her that a countdown of some sort was occurring, although she could not process exactly what kind. She was too busy replaying what Noah had said.

One word is all the permission I need to drop to my knees, lift your skirts, and have you riding my tongue until I have you coming apart.

Riding on his tongue? Did he mean like Katie was riding on Paul's cock? She could do that to Noah's tongue?

How... fascinating.

"John Richards," she whispered. "John Richards ca—"

"Can rot in hell," Noah growled, securing her tighter against him. The hard planes of his body felt right at home next to hers. "Going twice."

Willa looked around for signs of life but found none except the occasional flash of white from the waves crashing every so often.

"You wish to do it here?"

"Anywhere," he breathed, dipping his head to rub his nose against hers. "I will have you anyway, and anywhere you will allow me. All you have to do is say the word."

"What word am I supposed to say?" she asked stupidly. Even in the dark, when she could not see him clearly, everything about Noah Anderson befuddled her brain. "I don't know what to say."

He moved on from nuzzling her nose to brushing his lips over hers. Was this a kiss? Was she being kissed for the first time? The idea made her dizzy in the most fantastic way.

"Say yes, Willa."

Yes.

Say yes.

That's all she had to do.

And she could do it. She would do it. Allowing herself this one misstep in life.

"I have a request before I give my answer."

His breathing ragged, Noah nodded. "Ask, and it is yours."

"Will you allow me to get on my knees for you?" If she were going to do this, she wanted to experience it all. "Will you use my mouth as you described?"

The sound that tore from him was like nothing she had ever heard. A cross between a snarl and some sort of growl that was quickly cut off when his lips seized hers. A kiss. A real kiss. The brush of lips before was nothing but the prelude to the absolute destruction his mouth was now taking part in.

And he tasted divine.

Full lips worked against hers, urging them to part. When she did open, and his tongue slipped into her mouth, Willa held on to his shoulders, lifting on her toes as she sought more. She needed more—of him, of the kiss, of this terrible aching she didn't understand.

He walked her backward. One step at a time as he ravaged her mouth. They arrived at the forest's edge again, and Noah guided her to lean back on one of the sturdier tree trunks. Breaking the kiss, he stared down at her.

"I'll have your answer now."

She blinked several times, appreciating how her breathlessness didn't feel as if the end was near. It was the exact opposite. She felt alive. With every pump of her chest, she felt more powerful than before.

"You will explain everything as we go?"

That growl came from him again, and he braced a hand on the tree above her head. "Shall I begin now?"

She nodded, unable to look away from the burning blue, watching her intently. "Yes, please."

Licking his lips, Noah collected himself, sizing her up like a predator ready to pounce. "We'll start by you lifting your skirts."

"How high?"

"I want to see you—all of you," Noah said, pressing his forehead to hers. "I want to bask in the beauty I'm about to taste."

Nervous that her brother or anyone else might find them, she hesitated. It was completely dark, but the rising moon would provide enough light to allow someone to see.

"Wilhelmina." His fingers gripped her chin. "Be good."

She had never been the type to be obedient, but for Noah, she would be anything he asked.

Releasing his shoulders, her hands slowly lowered to her skirts.

"I'll be good." The cool air struck her stockinged legs first, and she shivered—not from the chill but from the smug look on Noah's face as she did as she was told. "But remember your promise."

"I won't forget."

Shifting back, he lowered himself to kneel on the sand and wait patiently as her skirt rose higher and higher.

"Tell me something," he murmured, his hands coming around to grip her calves. The warmth of his touch seeped through the material of her stockings, creating little wildfires along her skin as he moved upward. "Do you feel that wetness?"

He didn't have to explain further. She was acutely aware of her body and the manner of its response to his kiss.

She nodded mutely, and Noah chuckled. "May I taste it?"

"Um." Perhaps, she had not thought this through. "Um."

"May I bury my face between your legs and taste that sweetness waiting for me?" Biting down his grin, his gaze reluctantly rolled from her rising skirt to meet her own. "May I kiss the part of you made only for me?"

Heavens.

Reaching higher, his hands arrived at the backs of her thighs, and she almost dropped her skirt. The amused look on his face darkened, his fingers digging into the bare flesh at the top of her stockings. "Please, Willa."

It was the anticipation. Drawing tight in her lower belly, the anticipation was blocking out the world, leaving only them. The idea of his lips touching her intimately, his tongue... the things his tongue was going to do would end her right here on the beach.

And she would die a happy death.

"Do as you please, Dr. Anderson." Refusing to hide, she lifted her skirt as high as she could. "I am yours."

He started with a gentle brush of his lips on her upper thigh, the light grazing of his stubbled beard eliciting a gasp from her. Every muscle in her body went erect, and when she didn't think he could do anything else more erotic, the man went and ran his tongue along her flesh.

"So soft," he groaned, his hands continuing their trek higher until they were at the opening of her drawers. "The softest part of you, just as I suspected."

His dark head dipped, and the world stopped. An immediate halt. A flick. That's really all it was. A flick of his tongue brought everything to a standstill. Her heart. Her mind. Every part of her stood silent as his tongue tasted her.

Then he went and did it again.

Bliss. Extraordinary bliss like she had never known shot through her, and when Noah went to give her another swipe of the tongue, her fingers tangled in his hair.

"Noah…" Stars were popping in and out of her vision, and she squeezed her eyes shut, which only increased the rush as he worked his tongue and lips over her. "Noah."

He understood. Like a man who knew her body as well as she did, Noah understood what she wanted and increased the pressure of his movements. Falling back on the tree, Willa's legs spread wider while she rocked, the two of them finding a rhythm.

The languid strokes of his tongue became more deliberate as they moved, more insistent as he sought to discover exactly what she liked. And as her whimpers grew, Noah held her ass firmly, pulling her down on his face while he sucked with lips and teeth.

But when his tongue speared her center, seeking entrance, she shouted and lost herself entirely. The most obscene sounds rushed from her, and Willa vaguely thought of Paul and Katie on the shore. Except in her hedonistic mind, the image turned into Noah beneath her as she rode. His cock pumping deeply as she bounced on top of him.

"Don't fight it, Willa," Noah demanded, his voice muffled. "Relax."

She couldn't relax. Something was coming—something terrifyingly wanton and prowling inside, ready to rip from her body. The power behind it was like that of the sun. A bright and beautiful thing, unable to be denied.

Frightened, she fought its arrival, but then Noah slipped a finger inside her, curling and sliding it until the mysterious feeling tore free. Without warning, it struck, consuming her right there under the pines.

"Noah?" Bowing forward, she held his broad shoulders. Her body shook, her hips riding his finger while she moaned. "Noah, what is this?"

Being the tempting devil that he was, the man on his knees before her had the audacity to look up with a smug expression. His dark hair was a mess, falling forward across his brow while his eyes sparkled with male satisfaction.

"This is you falling in love, Wilhelmina Fairweather," he replied casually. Shifting back slightly, he took in the sight of her destruction, his finger continuing to help her chase the exquisite pleasure spreading like wildfire. "And I would suggest you get used to the feeling."

CHAPTER 12

S itting nestled between Noah's legs as they rode Hope back to Haven House, Willa shrugged off his attempted kiss. After her complete obliteration of morals on the beach, he had adjusted their clothing and informed her that it was time to go without giving her a chance to explore his body.

"I'm still angry," she snapped. The large hand flattened against her stomach glided up to cup a breast, and a sound between a groan and a gasp hissed through the night air. "You promised, Noah."

"Don't think I didn't want it." Teeth nipped at her ear, his playful nature becoming one of the most tantalizing things she had ever witnessed. "Don't think I didn't want to know what that razor-sharp tongue of yours could do."

They were far enough from the house that the dense forest still obscured them from view, and Willa turned in the saddle to shamelessly pout.

His expression darkened. "Oh, now that's not fair."

Cupping the back of her head, he kissed her, promptly quelling the disappointment with a slow glide of his tongue. In seconds, he had her aching all over again.

She shoved him half-heartedly away. "You are a beast, Noah Anderson."

"A beast?" He chuckled in the darkness. "Well, if anyone can tame a beast, it's you."

Tame him indeed. She had learned a few lessons on their ride, and wiggling her bottom, she caressed the painfully hard erection pressing into her back. Noah grunted and released a colorful string of explicit words.

"If you would have allowed me to get my hands," she boldly reached behind her, pressing her palm to the hard ridges she had yet to taste, "or mouth on you, this wouldn't be so painful."

Noah pressed his lips to her neck, his teeth scraping the line of muscle there. "Stop."

She didn't stop, craving to hear that hitch in his deep voice again. "I think I understand how it works," she whispered. "It wouldn't take long with you in this state, and the woods are thick. No one would see us."

"I need to get you home. It's well past dark, and our time is up." Air sawed roughly in and out of him, bringing him to an almost panting state. "Please stop, or I will do more than use your mouth."

Intrigued, her fingers gripped as much of him as they could through the material of his trousers. She had no idea how large the male anatomy could grow, but Noah was much bigger than the glimpse she caught of Paul.

"Such as?"

His head snapped up. Eyes wild with only the barest hint of control in them, his breathing turned shallow as she continued to move her hand. "I will use your body. Right here on the side of the road, I will use you in ways you cannot imagine, and I don't want to do that." His hips thrust forward, and he shuddered. "I don't want to have you like that the first time. I want you in a bed. Naked and with your legs spread wide when I fill you."

Willa's lips parted, her gaze holding his bravely. "Tell me more."

"I want you wanton and lost in your desire for me. As lost as I am whenever you are near." He groaned, his eyes closing as he continued to rock against her palm. "Your cries, Willa. I will own your cries. I will own your screams. All of you will belong to me. Forever."

Forever.

The word crossed his lips, and with it, a song rose on the wind. Coming in off the bayou far ahead, the sound had ice crystallizing in Willa's veins, flowing with its cold truth directly to her heart. A heart that could never be his, no matter how much it yearned to.

This was wrong. It wasn't fair to her, and it certainly wasn't fair to lead Noah into believing she was free to do as she pleased when she was just as trapped as Cal.

Sitting straight in the saddle, she spoke softly as she watched the sway of moss hanging high on the tunnel of oaks leading to Haven House. "You're right. Our time is up."

The heavy stream of Noah's breathing halted abruptly behind her. "Willa."

"Yes?"

"Look at me."

Tears stung, and she cursed herself. This was no one's fault but her own. She had allowed him in and, by doing so, had entangled them both thoroughly enough that the impending separation was going to cause unforgettable pain. All for a moment of pleasure. All for a memory she would cherish for a lifetime.

"I need to get back." Holding on to Hope's mane, she kept facing forward. "My parents will begin to worry if I'm out too far past sunset. I've never done such a thing."

"Willa."

She didn't need to turn to know her name was being uttered through clenched teeth, and when she ignored him again, Noah swung down off Hope's back.

"We're walking the rest of the way."

"I would rather ride, thank you."

Noah's large hand landed on her thigh and squeezed. "Get off the horse, Willa."

Head high, she scrambled to maintain the small shred of dignity left in her and remained seated on the horse. "I'm feeling rather winded and would like to rid—eeek!" Wide-eyed, she tried to kick him away when he tickled her inner thigh. "Do not do that!"

Refusing to cease his torment of her leg, Noah bared his teeth as he ordered her yet again. "Then get off the damn horse."

"Fine," she huffed, swinging her leg over to dismount. This time around, she got off the horse with much more agility than she knew she possessed and stood before him with her hands on her hips. "Happy?"

Yanking her to him, he snarled a single word before capturing her mouth. "No."

The kisses before this one were playful, exploratory even. Soft and lingering, they allowed her to learn as they went. He hadn't pushed her out of feeling anything but comfort, permitting her to lead, which was probably why she lost her head.

But this kiss…This kiss was nothing like the others. It wasn't playful, soft, or slow. It was greedy, a desperate claim that screamed his intentions.

And she couldn't stop herself from responding in kind. This man was everything she had ever dreamed of. A fantasy come to life. Kind, caring, and able to let her fly as only he could, Noah held her trust, and Wilhelmina Fairweather never trusted anyone.

"You will not cut me out," he growled as she clung to him for more. "You will not get lost in that extraordinary mind of yours. It overthinks everything, and while I usually marvel at the way it works, I'll not allow it to push me away."

It wasn't as if she could stop her tears and let them fall. "Noah…"

"No."

No.

And he thought she was the stubborn one. He uttered the word as if he could change their circumstances with his will alone.

Holding them pressed together, he rested his forehead on hers, and she didn't try to pull away, too desperate for the intimacy.

"If you could have any future, what would it be?" he asked. "A husband? A home?"

Ah, so he meant to emotionally ruin her before the evening was over. How delightful.

"It doesn't matter."

"What you want is all that matters," he said, determined to make her see things his way. "Now answer me. What kind of future? A life with Richards? A life here at Haven House? If you could choose anything, what would it be?"

Afraid she would become even more distraught if she spoke, Willa shook her head.

"Say it." His nostrils flared at her refusal to speak. "Please."

He was begging, and seeing him do so might be the end of her yet. "If I were free, I would not want those things," she replied, her voice barely above a whisper.

When she didn't continue, Noah brushed his lips across hers. "Tell me."

Could she do it?

Could she say it out loud?

He might laugh.

But what if he didn't?

Scrunching her face tight, she spoke the truth. "You."

As if coming out of a nightmare, the tension on Noah's face lessened. "*Me.*"

Her mouth worked to form what she wanted to say, but even with her brain racing to articulate a reply, it didn't matter. The truth all came tumbling out anyway. "I want you. I want to be with you. If I could have any future, I would have one with you. A life. A home. Children?" She took a shaky inhale as the gravity of what she was confessing struck her fully. "And I want what happened on the beach to happen every day."

"Every day?" Her wicked man returned with his carefree smirk at the ready. "My, my, I have my work cut out for me."

"And I want more." If she were going to burn in eternal damnation, she might as well arrive at the pits of hell good and well on fire from embarrassment. "I want to do to you what Katie was doing to Paul. I want to be in control yet completely under your power."

Noah's head lowered, his lips and tongue tracing the column of her neck. "Continue," he ordered. "Don't stop now."

"I want you in my mouth and between my legs," she went on. Her fingers tangled in his hair, holding him close when the scrape of his canine met her flesh. "I want you to fill me and give me babies. I want to be your wife, Noah Anderson. The only woman you love."

He backed her up, hiding them in the forest directly off the drive. "I do believe you just proposed to me, Ms. Fairweather." Her back landed against a tree with a thud, and Noah stared down at her in a wholly possessive way. "And if that is the case, I accept."

Willa's knees promptly buckled. He could not mean it. He could not possibly mean to whisk her away. She didn't deserve it. Not when her sister would be crushed by Paul's betrayal.

"Lucy."

"I know she'll be upset about Paul, but I have an idea. She's been writing to Mr. Richards on your behalf?"

"Yes?"

"And after what I've witnessed and from what you've told me, I assume they've become friends?"

"Noah..."

"And your family wants the land John Richards is willing to provide should he receive a wife."

He looked like a boy. This utterly masculine man looked as giddy as a child who had concocted the perfect plan for creating mischief. "I know where you're going with this, but Lucy does honestly love Paul. She won't want another man. Not even one she considers a friend."

Leaning in, Noah nipped at her bottom lip. "Your sister is kind and decent. A genuinely good person."

"There is no need to sell me on the merits of my sister." She yanked him closer by his vest, both smiling like a pair of co-conspirators. "I know how wonderful she is."

"Then let us show John Richards how wonderful she is."

Utterly uninhibited, she kissed him for being a genius. "If I recall, it was you who suggested that she write him in the first place since I was always so busy with my doctor visits."

"Amazing how that worked out."

Smacking his chest, she pretended to be shocked, but ended up laughing her head off. "Amazing, indeed."

Noah turned serious, observing her in the moonlight. "I want you like this always."

"Like what?"

"Happy." He raised his hand hesitantly, toying with the ends of her chestnut strands. "Can I have you like this, Willa? Can I have you like this forever? With your hair down, your face flushed, and your lips swollen from my kisses?"

He had her standing on that mountaintop again. The very same one he had led her to during The Gathering. "Yes."

"By Christmas."

The massive smile on her face flattened into a line of disbelief. "What?"

"I want you to be my wife before Christmas."

"Christmas is in three weeks!" Her heart pounded in her chest, the excitement over what he was saying made her woozy. "We cannot convince Mr. Richards to marry Lucy and plan to run away together before Christmas."

Running away together? It sounded so romantic. However, when dealing with her father, the idea was less like what she would find in one of her romances and more like a gothic novel coming to life.

"Why would we have to leave?" He was genuinely confused, and it broke her heart. "Don't you want to be married with your family in attendance?"

"My father will never approve." If he were truly willing to take her on, it was best if he understood the way of things. "Of you, I mean. Not when you can give him nothing in return. He would rather I rot away in that house than give up a possession for free."

"Fine. Let him win. But then again, I can't think of a better story to tell our children one day. Who wouldn't want to hear of how their father was so desperate for their mother that he stole her away in the night?" Seizing her by the hips with two hands, he massaged the muscles there. "I want us to go up north. I think your lungs will do much better in cooler weather."

"But what if I don't?" She chewed on her bottom lip, thinking the whole thing through. "What if I'm worse?"

"Then we'll go to a drier one and continue moving until we find a climate that works for you," he replied as if he had already planned it. "The tea leaves I mentioned have arrived and are in my pocket. We can try them during your next attack and keep them on hand as we travel."

He had yet to witness her in the throes of a breathing spell. Not that she minded, but she was afraid Noah would think she wasn't worth the hassle once he did.

"I can't ask you to move all over the place."

The hands on her hips shifted to her rear and squeezed. "You can ask anything of me, and I'll give it to you."

"Oh, really?" His erection rubbed against her belly, and she swayed her hips. "Can I start by asking for this? Tonight?"

The blasted man took a step to the side. "Not tonight."

"Tomorrow night?" She hoped she didn't sound too eager, but patience was not one of her virtues. "Please?"

He turned serious. "Do you think you can sneak out tomorrow night?"

She nodded, having done it a few times as a child. It had been during those never-ending years when her family had been so sure she would drop dead if she stepped outside, and the only way to receive fresh air was to sneak off in the middle of the night. "As long as the staff and Bonnie haven't changed their nighttime routine, I should be in the clear just after midnight."

"Then I will come for you at midnight." Taking her hand, he led them back to Hope waiting on the lane. "Watch for my signal from the forest."

CHAPTER 13

The following night, it wasn't very hard to stay up until midnight. Excitement wouldn't allow her to rest, but just before the clock struck twelve, the faint sound of Grace's song could be heard. Realizing it wasn't coming from the house, Willa stepped onto the balcony. She was already dressed to go, wearing a white nightgown covered by one of Cal's dark wool coats that felt almost two sizes too big for her.

Standing in the night air, a feeling of peace settled over her as she listened. The fog lay thick across Haven's grounds, with no life or movement to be seen except for the slow roll of mist coasting its way up from the bayou to blanket the estate. In just a few days, the loggers would fully depart for the holiday break, and her mother and Bonnie had spent the day decorating Haven House for Christmas, leaving nary a banister or window frame without a wreath or bow of holly. Everything had to be perfect for Stephen Fairweather's long days spent at home. They might not entertain during the holidays, but he expected the house to appear as though they did.

John Richards had called upon them in the late morning hours, directly amid the decorating chaos. Normally, his arrival would have caused an issue, but Willa managed to wrangle him into helping.

And straight into Lucy's path.

The tree was Lucy's domain. Every ornament and strand of tinsel had a proper place, and she excelled at creating a picturesque scene in the parlor. More than a little too eagerly, John Richards offered her his assistance, and the two of them toiled the afternoon away, chatting and laughing as they worked.

Her mother was too busy directing staff and the Port Michaelson girls to notice Willa purposely making herself scarce while Lucy and John Richards spent time together.

However, there was no fooling Bonnie.

Like a hawk, Bonnie watched, volleying between helping Margaret direct the staff and minding everyone else's affairs. She fussed at Jennie, who continuously made excuses to find her way into the library where Cal was hard at work on something for the mill. She fussed after Willa, relentlessly urging her to join her sister and John Richards in the parlor.

But in the end, it all worked out to where Willa didn't have to worry about sneaking out. Bonnie and her mother exhausted themselves and everyone else before the day was over. The holiday season was officially here, and with her father preparing to be home more thanks to the mill's holiday break, Haven House had to be perfect.

In the moonlight, Willa shivered and waited patiently for Noah's signal. She didn't have to wait long. The glow of a lantern appeared across the lane, flashing once and then twice, it alerted her that it was time.

Slipping from her room, Willa snuck onto the landing without making a sound. She listened for a second and, when hearing nothing, dashed down the stairs to creep silently to the front door.

Once she made it to the porch, a surge of relief hit over how effortlessly her escape had been, and she chuckled to herself as she closed the front door softly behind her.

"Willa?"

Willa stumbled back into the shadows, sucking in a sharp gasp as she did.

Cal emerged from the dark, his shirt open and hair a mess. "What are you doing out here?" he whispered. "Go back inside."

"What am *I* doing out here?" she hissed, waving a hand at his exposed chest. "What are *you* doing out here?"

A figure shifted behind Cal, and Willa arched an eyebrow, peering around her brother to get a better look. "Good evening, Jennie."

Jennie peeked over Cal's shoulder. Dressed in a white nightgown, she was the very essence of beauty and health. A perfect picture of everything Willa wanted to be.

"Good evening, Ms. Willa." Sliding her hands around Cal's body, Jennie embraced him without shame. "How are you?"

Yes, you could see this girl was special. The world likely loved her without question, allowing dear Jennie to shine. It was an easy thing to see, especially when you were the exact opposite and left to dwell in the shallow end of life.

"That's a lovely nightgown," Willa said to Jennie, meaning it. The delicate floral details sewn into the garment were unique and quite pretty. "Did you make it yourself?"

Jennie shook her head, her luxurious loose mane of thick sandy brown hair flowing around her shoulders. "My mother made it for me right before she died."

"Oh, I'm so sorry to hear of your mother's passing."

"It happened over a year ago," Jennie replied, seemingly indifferent on the matter. "My parents died in a fire at our home. I was in Port Michaelson helping my sick aunt with her dairy farm when we got the word, so I simply never left."

Cal reached behind him, holding Jennie with one arm. "The aunt died directly before The Gathering, and Jennie has nowhere else to go for now."

Eyeballing her brother, Willa kept her expression neutral. When Noah mentioned Cal was falling for this Jennie girl, it had been a laughable idea. Her brother was hardly serious about anything, let alone the women he courted. One after another, he would entertain himself with various females both while at home and even more so—as Willa had heard from Bonnie—during his semesters away at college.

"Well, there is always work to be done at Haven House, and we're happy to have you, Jennie."

Directly across the way, the glowing light of Noah's lantern flashed impatiently in the woods.

"Who is that?" Cal went to the porch railing, lifting on his toes as if it would help him see through the fog better. "Are you meeting someone?"

He sounded utterly aghast at the thought. As if she could never have a suitor waiting for a secret rendezvous.

And it grated.

"I am."

Her brother's shoulders shook while he quietly laughed. "You're joking."

Head high, she made her way to the steps. "I trust you will keep this conversation between us." She nodded a goodnight at Jennie. "As will I."

Cal rushed over to block her way with a giggling Jennie right at his side. The lightheartedness in his expression was gone, and he coldly glared down at Willa in a way that reminded her of their father.

"Who?"

Willa didn't answer, keeping her gaze averted.

"If you don't tell me, I'll not let you go." Cal gripped her chin painfully, forcing her to face him. "Richards? It's an awfully long trek from Hollingsdale to have a secret rendezvous."

"It's not Mr. Richards."

"Then, wh—" As realization dawned, Cal released his hold on her chin. "Well, that explains it."

Willa glared at him. "Explains what?"

Cal's eyes slid from her face to Jennie, a gaping smile spreading. "Things."

Willa didn't care to be made fun of and pinched her brother's bare chest, pleased when he yelped. "What things?"

"He never stays." Rubbing the reddening spot on his rib cage, Cal draped an arm across Jennie's shoulders. "For our parties."

Jennie's adorably freckled face lit up. "Oh, the doctor," she whispered with excitement. "That does explain why he always ignored poor Ruth whenever she tried to have a... um, conversation with him."

Willa had no clue who Ruth was but hated the woman instantly. "Goodnight, Cal."

"Willa, wait."

She paused on the first step, losing her nerve by the second. Her brother nodded at Noah's lantern. The light was almost fully obscured by the fog now. "Be back by three. Father wakes at four whether he's going to the mill or not."

"Although he has been slow to wake lately," Jennie added eagerly. "But I guess it depends on how much he exerts himself in the night."

A flicker of annoyance crossed Cal's face, but it quickly vanished into nothing. "The ground is soggy this late, and if you're going where I think you're going, those boots of yours will be covered in mud once you return. Make sure to take them off before coming up the porch steps so you don't leave tracks. You can hide them in the bushes and retrieve them later in the day when no one is paying attention."

Surprised he was willing to help, Willa nodded. "Thank you."

"Loose ends, Willa." Cal went serious again. "Always tie them up."

She said goodnight and rushed off, disappearing into the mist. Following the light as it grew brighter, she almost crashed into Noah when she found him.

"Cal stopped me," she said between his kisses. "But he let me go."

"Cal has no room to judge." Laying one last quick kiss upon her lips, Noah took her hand and began leading them deep into the forest by way of the trail that led to the Anderson estate. "We're going to my medical cottage."

"Can we..." She paused, nearly wrapping herself at his side. The forest at night always brought back memories she never wanted to relive. "Will we have privacy?"

He flashed a smile over his shoulder. "Worried you might scream as you did on the beach?"

There was no demure blushing this time, with Willa being completely comfortable. Noah had placed the impossible idea of being his wife in her head, and she had seized the dream with both hands. "I'm honestly hoping I scream louder."

"You will," he assured her.

"I spent the day cleaning and straightening everything." He closed and locked the door before turning on the desk's gas lamp. The remodel on the cottage had gone exceedingly well, with Noah having a small examination room and even a pair of beds for those patients he might need to monitor overnight. "I wanted this to be perfect for you."

Willa stood at the door, watching as Noah showed her items that had been added since her last visit. The man was so very capable in every way, but appeared nervous at the moment, and she took her time marveling at the change.

He stopped abruptly in the middle of the room, rubbing a hand on the back of his neck. "Never in my life have I ever been unsure of how to begin something like this."

Willa approached slowly with her hands clasped tightly in front of her. "And just how many women have you seduced, Dr. Anderson?"

"More than I'd care to admit." He smiled sheepishly. "But none of them will be remembered after you."

"I would hope not." Standing before him, she smoothed her hands over his shoulders. He was wearing a simple dress shirt and wool pants. All of which needed to be removed. Post haste. He had promised he would allow her to explore his body, and Willa was anxious to learn every detail. "I am to be your wife, after all."

He released a sigh as if relieved. "What I feel for you can't be explained, and my greatest passion is to find the explanation for everything. A cause to the end result. But with you, I have been categorically and infinitely enchanted since the moment we met." Crystal blue eyes searched hers, the depths of them holding her captive. "My body. My soul. They're yours, and I can't explain it. I only know that they are yours, Willa."

Not needing to hear anymore, she shed her coat, allowing it to drop to the floor. Her long nightgown was next, and she tossed it onto the desk chair. Naked and not at all afraid, Willa released the pins from her hair, allowing it to fall over her shoulders. "Then take what is yours."

"Dear God." Noah drank her in, pulling back a step to see her fully. "The things I'm going to do to you." He swiped a hand over his mouth, moving around her in a circle as his eyes coasted over her nude form. "The way I'm going to make you feel."

"But will I scream?" she teased, enjoying this sway she held over him. No man had ever yearned for her like this, let alone a man like Noah. "Will you give me that again?"

He was behind her when she asked, and Willa found herself snatched back against his chest. "I'm going to give you more." Lips and tongue coasted along the spot where her neck met her shoulder, and she sighed, relishing the secure hold around her waist. "Are you ready to begin?"

"I am."

"Are you going to do as I say?"

"Probably not."

A laugh rumbled from somewhere deep inside him. "At least I'll never have to worry about your honesty."

Turning slowly, she stood in his arms, her naked body pressed to his clothed one. "I'll never lie to you," she promised as his hands glided lower to grip her bottom. "But will you please remove your clothes now? I'm feeling a bit awkward being the only nude one in the room."

He smiled and staring at the genuine affection shining brightly down on her, Willa knew one thing for certain.

They were going to have a wonderful life.

A beautiful one.

Together.

Noah would keep her safe as she would him. They would care for one another until the end of their lives, and then maybe even longer if the powers above granted it.

"You look so serious, Ms. Fairweather," he whispered. "What are you thinking about?"

"Sonnet forty-three."

He thought for a second or two, and as understanding struck, the carefree smile on his full lips faltered. "*I love thee with the breath, smiles, tears, of all my life; and, if God choose, I shall but love thee better after death?*"

Death lurked like a menacing figure in her life, watching and waiting for her to become weak enough to steal away. Reminders of her mortality were tucked into every corner of Haven House. From her beloved conservatory to the second-floor expansive balcony she could hardly ever enjoy to Grace's bedroom right next door. Death was always there.

But with Noah, she wasn't afraid. Death could chase her for eternity, and with him at her side, Willa felt as if she would have the courage to wave the grim reaper off, telling it to return another day.

"I was thinking about how we're going to have a good life," she replied as casually as she could. It was hard to remain this happy while utterly terrified at the same time. "I never thought someone like you would happen to someone like me. I never thought that a handsome man, who is a doctor *and* knows Browning sonnets *but yet* unfortunately prefers Keats to Shelly—"

"My taste is impeccable."

She swatted his chest. "—Could walk through the door of Haven House—"

"And sweep you directly off your feet with nothing but my charm and a stethoscope." He shrugged, the smile she loved returning. "Admittedly, I am a talented man."

"With a tremendous ego."

"A warranted ego." His dark head dipped for him to whisper in her ear. "Just look at how you're pressed against my body. Naked and waiting patiently for me to ravage you. The great Wilhelmina Fairweather. Brilliant and beautiful, and all mine."

Noah's large hand skated up her body to massage a breast, and she arched her back for more. "Your clothes."

He led them over to a full-length clawed foot mirror in the corner. The piece looked as if it belonged in a grand manor and not a makeshift hospital in the middle of the forest. Then again, most of the adornments, from the desk to the cabinets and even the bed in the corner, likely came from the Andersons' home. Cal had said Noah's aunt and uncle were doing everything they could to tempt him to stay on past the winter.

Her cheeks heated as they stood in front of the mirror, her body on full display. Understanding, Noah turned to face the mirror, blocking her view to where she could see nothing but him and her eyes peeking over his shoulder.

"Undress me."

Tentatively, she reached around to unbutton his pants, and Noah chuckled. "Going straight for the best part, eh?"

Willa shrunk behind his shoulder, hiding her embarrassment. "Curiosity and all that."

"Well, go on then." He quickly unbuttoned his shirt and shucked it off. "Continue being curious."

She would, if not so shocked. In the mirror, Noah's broad chest nearly filled the entire thing, reflecting back at her in all its glory. Muscled and toned, with the barest hint of dark hair scattered across it, he waited as she gawked.

"Willa?"

"A moment if you please." Unable to stop herself, she kept her gaze locked on the image of him. Pressing her lips to the bare flesh of his shoulder, she had an overwhelming urge to taste his skin. "You are beautiful, Noah."

Patient while she touched him, he permitted her to run her hands over every sculpted muscle on his chest and abdomen. The light dusting of hair tickled her palms, and she followed it to the spot just below his navel.

"Willa, I can't wait much longer," he breathed, and she sank her teeth into his shoulder, causing Noah to growl low in his throat. "You've gone and done it now."

Reaching behind him, he sought the growing wetness between her thighs. Without hesitating, she spread her stance, giving him access. The pads of his fingers connected with the throbbing ache begging for him, her hips rolling in time with the circular motions of his touch.

"Stroke me, Willa."

He worked his pants lower, already undone from her previous work. As his shaft broke free, her mouth fell open involuntarily.

"How... how..." She released a little moan when his finger edged inside her. "Will you show me how I should do this?"

Using his free hand, he guided her to touch him lower. "Hold me."

One at a time, she wrapped her fingers delicately around his cock. It was so very hard. Smooth in some sections, with a large head and lengthy shaft.

Covering her hand with his, he guided her, conveying exactly how to pump his cock as they watched in the mirror.

"When I'm inside you, the tight channel of your body will hold me," he said, the explanation dripping with raw desire. "I'll move my hips, similar to how Paul did with Katie. The sliding motion creates friction."

Willa loved him a little more for knowing she needed to hear the exact details. "Why friction?"

"Because it feels good." His eyes shuttered, his hips thrusting with each stroke of their hands. "The slickness of your arousal will allow me to build speed until the heavy slam of my body into yours builds."

Breathless from both his ministrations between her legs and the way he was reacting to her touch, Willa shook her head to clear it. "Builds into what?"

"Screaming."

"Will you scream?"

A shaky laugh left him. "I think I might."

"What if I use my mouth?" she asked, truly wanting to know how to make this good for him. "Would that make you scream?"

She released his length when he didn't reply and stepped between him and the mirror. "Tell me how to do it."

He seemed uncertain. "I don't think that's a good idea this time around."

"Why not?" She pushed at his pants, easing them further down his thighs. "Let me."

A blush tinted his cheeks. "Control when it comes to you... do you understand what happens when a man finishes?"

Unfortunately, when Bonnie had given her and Grace a speech about marital affairs, they had giggled throughout the entire thing leaving the end slightly hazy.

"I think so?"

"Ah, well, I would likely finish in your mouth. I don't think I could stop myself."

This whole side of Noah was fascinating, and it had her slowly sinking to the floor, her nails scratching across his skin as she fell. "Then don't."

"Willa." Her name snagged in his throat as he watched her settle on her knees. "Not for long."

A drop of moisture beaded at his impressive tip, and she licked her lips, examining every ridge and vein straining under her observation. "When you say stop, I will."

Stop what exactly? She didn't know. She had never seen what to do, so she decided to do what she wanted. With a flick of her tongue, she lapped at the wetness, waiting.

Noah hissed, and she paused before going in for another taste. "Am I doing something wrong?"

He shook his head, chest rising and falling rapidly. "Hold me like you were a moment ago and pump. Slowly." She did as he instructed, noticing the goosebumps covering his thighs. "Now take me into your mouth, sucking slightly as you do."

When her lips closed around him, a loud moan broke from Noah. She relished the sound, and while it took her a few tries to become accustomed to the sensation of having him in her mouth, she found it easier after setting a comfortable rhythm.

"Ah, God." His fingers tangled in her hair, and she increased her speed, timing the bob of her head with the plunge of his cock into her mouth. "I want to be gentle with you." His hips thrust forward, gagging her slightly. "But I don't know that I can."

She released him to catch her breath but kept a steady pace with her hand. "It's going to hurt, isn't it?"

"I'll be good to you, Willa." Noah let out another groan, louder this time, and she returned her mouth to his cock, unable to stop herself from sucking him in as far as she could go. When his tip grazed the back of her throat, the muscles on his stomach shivered. "But yes, it will hurt."

She came up for air a second time, panting as heavily as him. "And never again?"

"Never again."

Pressing a goodbye kiss to his thick shaft, she stood. "Well, then, I'm ready to get the painful part out of the way."

CHAPTER 14

On a trip to Hollingsdale once, Willa ventured into the rear section of the local bookshop. As with every visit to town, her mother permitted her to purchase as many books as she could carry.

The gesture was not out of kindness. It was done only because Margaret knew that the more her daughter read, the more likely Willa would stay hidden in her conservatory and leave the rest of them alone.

So, when she wandered into the little bookshop off Main Street that day, her family left her to her own devices, as did the shop's proprietor, who understood both Willa's ailments and that she was never truly permitted much freedom away from Haven House.

And that was how she ended up in the rear of the bookshop. A secret corner where the more risqué selections could be found. Nothing too untoward, of course. A sordid romance here or there, and perhaps an art book where the sketches involved nudity.

It was one of the art books Willa had dared to open. Skimming the pages as her cheeks reddened, she absorbed as much as she could. The beautiful women in their many shapes and sizes, the men with their heated gazes and blatant arousals, and the sketches of them copulating vigorously on various pieces of furniture.

All of it had seemed so scandalously delicious, and she had returned the book to the shelf, disappointedly secure in the fact that she would never experience such a moment.

Oh, how wrong she had been.

Laying on the small bed, her feet firmly planted on the mattress and legs spread as she waited, Willa stretched her arms over her head. "Are you going to tease me like this for the rest of the night?"

Eyes on her breasts, Noah remained kneeling between her thighs, stroking himself. "I'm attempting to get myself under control, or this will end quicker than I would like," he murmured. "Have you ever touched yourself?"

She knew exactly what he meant, and in her current state, Willa didn't think she could become any more self-conscious, so she answered truthfully. "Yes."

"Did you enjoy it?"

"Not as much as what you did to me in the forest."

"Do it now," he demanded, his gaze dropping to that pulsing heat waiting. "I want to see."

Lowering her hand, she mimicked his movements from when they stood in front of the mirror. Tiny circles of pressure served to soak her fingers and drive her hips upward as her body sought to be filled.

Noah watched intently, and with cock in hand, he leaned forward to rub the tip along her opening. He groaned, edging her with the promise of entering. "Would you like me to use my tongue?"

Willa nodded enthusiastically. But that wasn't good enough for Noah.

"Answer me." His free hand latched onto her thigh, holding her still. The motion of his cock increased, burying itself a little further. "You are drenched and ready, but do you want me to taste you first? Do you want my tongue inside you, Willa?"

"Yes."

He was on her in seconds. Feasting as if she were his final meal. Her own fingers were knocked away as he devoured her in the most explicitly carnal way possible. The pleasure built under the assault, gaining speed and quickening in her belly. She swore loudly and lifted her hips just as his eyes rolled up in his head.

"Oh, God, I'm going to..." The wave prepared to crash down on her. Rising high and ready to obliterate as he sucked her tender flesh between his teeth. "*Scream.*"

"Not yet." Abruptly ending his work, Noah covered her with his body to settle between her legs. "On my cock," he growled, notching inside her once more. "I want to feel this cunt holding me when you fall apart."

To hear such vulgar language only spurned her on, and she clung to him, gasping as he filled her. The pain sliced for but a second, her mind registering it briefly as her body contracted.

"*I... Noah...*"

He struggled to be careful while she groaned, holding still as the stinging pain merged with an undeniable pleasure. "Holy hell," she whimpered, the muscles in her body drawing tight as he began to move at an achingly slow pace. "Deeper. I want you deeper, Noah."

Lifting up on his arms, Noah stared at her with a ferocious love burning in his gaze. "Hold on to me," he panted, his labored breaths making him hoarse. "I'll give you what you need."

Obeying, she gripped his waist, and their tempo accelerated. The steady drum of his hips colliding with hers had Willa moving with him. Moans carried through the air, the harmonious sound driving her to widen her legs and give him room to move.

The bed's metal headboard banged loudly against the plank wall, and its squeaking mattress wasn't doing much better against their attack. Sweet release chased her again, crawling across her skin as it sought freedom. It promised a cataclysmic demise, pulling at the very fabric of her being.

"Don't stop, Noah."

And Noah appeared to have no intention of doing any such thing. His parted lips curved upward as he filled her with a heavy ramming, striking the place inside where she needed it most. "Give it to me, Willa. Give me what's mine."

Holding his supple ass with clawed fingers, she bounced beneath him, riding every hit with greedy abandon. "Anything."

That's when it happened. The end of Wilhelmina Fairweather. The woman she once was evaporated into nothing, wiped away by the unmatched bliss coursing through her. She screamed his name—louder than she had ever screamed. She swore. She begged. She thrashed and convulsed, dying the most beautiful of deaths.

"So, good." Noah's own broken shouts joined hers. "You feel so good, Willa."

A trembling took over, diving down to her very center, and the tempo of his thrusts changed. Rolling his hips, he worked at burying himself completely. "Take all of me love," he grunted. "I know you can."

And she did. Bringing her knees to her chest, she opened her legs as Noah held her thighs to ride her with lengthy pumps of his cock.

"That's it." Above her, Noah's large frame shook, his thrusting turning erratic. He let out a shout as he lost a little more control over himself. "Ah, God, that's it, Willa."

Her greedy body squeezed around him, wanting everything he was giving. She had no idea how she had lived without this—without him—for as long as she had. Noah was the other half of her soul and to survive without him would be impossible from this day forward.

The muscles in his stomach shivered as the shouts crossing his lips turned to moans. "Are you my woman?"

"Yes," she cried, losing herself yet again to him. She understood what to expect this time and relaxed, welcoming the annihilation with fevered excitement. "I'm yours."

"Are you going to be my wife?"

The question catapulted them both over the edge, and Noah spilled into her, his cock pulsing and bringing her own end exploding forth. She gave her reply in the middle of it, forever fusing their lives together.

"No one will ever take you from me." He collapsed on top of her when it was over, kissing her leisurely as he made promises she knew he would keep until their dying days. "You are forever mine, Willa."

They lay in the dark, facing each other, hands and lips exploring. Sweat cooled their skin, creating a comfortable enough temperature for them to lie naked atop the blankets.

"Men shouldn't be so beautiful." She traced the etched muscles of his chest with her fingertips. "But you are."

Nibbling on her neck, he palmed a breast. "Do I need to take you back over to the mirror?" he asked. "Bend you over in front of it and have you from behind just so you can watch how beautiful *you* are." He sunk his teeth into her flesh. "Especially when taking my cock."

Take her from behind? She shivered at the thought. "Such language, Dr. Anderson."

Leaving a trail of kisses down to her breasts, he swirled his tongue over a nipple, teasing it into a peak. "You like hearing me say cock."

"I like you using it, too."

Dropping a delicate kiss on one breast before moving to another, Noah continued to learn her body. His hands hadn't stopped moving since they finished, as if he were memorizing every line and curve with his touch.

Willa giggled when his teeth scraped a ticklish spot. This couldn't be real. This moment was like a dream she'd dreamt a thousand times. A fantasy she'd concocted in her head to get through the days of being so lonely.

"When you say *take me from behind*, do you mean like an animal?"

He planted a kiss on her stomach before looking up and casually rubbing his stubbled chin against her skin. "With a little more skill, I hope, but yes, it's the same concept."

A thought took over, and she couldn't stop it from coming out of her mouth. She had already asked, but... "Have you done what we just did with many women?"

Noah worked his way back up her body, settling on top of her so they could be face to face. "A few, but I cannot say it was anything like what we just did."

She didn't want to know. Really. "How so?"

"Before you, it was only to fulfill a need."

"And after me?"

"There is only you." He kissed her, their tongues seeking to match each stroke of the others with perfect synchronicity. "There will only be you."

Holding him close as they took their time enjoying the moment, she listened as he told her of his plans. They would go to Ohio first and see if she handled the change.

"And you'll get to see snow for the first time."

"I beg your pardon." She faked outrage, batting her lashes at him. "I've seen snow before, and we even went down to the beach to watch it mix with the powder sand."

He grinned, that boyishness coming over him again. "That sounds strange but oddly beautiful."

They continued to discuss their future, talking about his parents and how they would hopefully be able to visit them in the spring.

"My parents are going to love you, Willa."

"Why can't we go meet them first?" she asked. "Why do you want to go to Ohio when they live in Indiana?"

"A man named Edward Parsons is a doctor in Ohio. I worked under him and have been writing to him about your case," he told her. "He once treated an entire family of asthmatics quite successfully. All twenty-something of them have gone on to live fully under his care."

A full life.

With Noah.

"That sounds amazing."

"Dr. Parsons had actually offered me a job directly before I came down here, and if you do well in the area of his practice, I mean to take him up on it." He rubbed his nose against hers. "So, tell me, Wilhelmina Fairweather. Will you be content being the wife of a lowly Ohio doctor?"

She pretended to think on the matter. "I'm not sure, but I will try my best."

"Oh, will you?" He tickled her ribs, eliciting a squeal. "Well, I will have to do my best to keep you satisfied."

Willa wrapped her legs around him. "I can think of a few ways you can keep me satisfied," she said.

"No, you harlot," he teased. "You'll be too sore, and I don't want to hurt you."

"But I would very much like to do more screaming," she confessed, prepared to beg shamelessly. "Can we do other things?"

"Oh, absolutely."

CHAPTER 15

"Are you sure you want to just run off and not speak to your parents first?"

They were standing at the edge of the forest with Haven House resting quietly just beyond the lane. Willa felt what was now becoming a familiar jolt of terror whenever she thought of running off. She wondered if Grace had felt the same and how she'd overcome that raw fear.

"My parents would never understand." He'd given further details of his family as they talked between their more intimate moments. Noah's parents sounded lovely and quite normal—nothing at all like her own. "I'm sorry."

"I only hate for them to lose two daughters the same way."

Movement caught her eye in the dense forest behind him, and Willa stared at it. "They won't."

His large hand cupped her cheek, and he watched her intently, likely concerned with how pale she'd gone. "Are you able to breathe?"

Able to breathe? With him? Noah allowed her to fly—to soar—higher than she ever dreamed. Her eyes searched the void of darkness forming behind him, wanting it to understand how in love she was with this man. How she could never survive without him.

"I love you very much, Noah."

Winding her arms around his neck, Willa kissed him, not wanting the night to end just yet. They had a few more minutes until the clock struck three, and the comforting pressure of his mouth on hers was all she needed to get through.

But then the song began softly.

Carrying through the midnight black of the forest, it mingled with the wind, gently tossing the branches above their heads. She had found peace in Grace's song earlier, but now, with what would become the most monumental decision of her life looming, that peace shifted into dread as she finally understood.

Grace's song.

A lullaby.

First sung by Bonnie, it was a melody for newborn babes, warning of life's tumultuous paths should they not obey their parents. It was a tune each of them knew by heart, but Grace made the song beautiful with her enchanting voice.

Ending their kiss, Willa held Noah tight, keeping him as the only thing in her line of sight. "Can you hear her?"

His brows knitted together as he listened. "Jennie and Cal must be in the forest."

"That's not Jennie singing."

He felt it then, his eyes going wide. The darkness. The past returning to haunt them. It was curious, pressing in to get a better look. To his credit, Noah stood perfectly still, his grip on her becoming like a vice.

"I lied to you," Willa whispered. "We've lied to everyone."

His gaze slid to the right as if assessing what was coming up from behind. "Willa?"

"I'm so sorry, Noah." She was crying, careful and controlled, just as she was taught. No hysterics else someone might hear. "They were running away, and *he* found them."

The song faltered, dissolving into nothing as it listened, reliving the memory with her.

"Grace and Tommy," she went on. "They were going to live at his mother's home in Atlanta until Tommy could find work far from our mill, but *he* found out."

A chill encircled where they stood, distinct and shapeless. Noah pulled her further into his arms, and the wool of Cal's coat itched along her neck. "What are you telling me?"

She shouldn't allow him to hold her when she was about to speak a truth that might have him giving up this entire idea of making her his wife. She could have been deceitful and waited until they were wed before revealing it, but that wasn't fair. He needed to know. Noah had to understand what they were up against and why there would be no going back when she did finally escape Haven House.

"My father."

There was a tickle on the back of her wrist, ghostly fingertips tracing the freckled pattern that matched its own. The touch pushed her to be brave, reminding her that the possibility of a life with Noah was worth the risk.

"Grace knew my father would never accept her choice. I've told you she was beautiful. Men throughout this county and all the neighboring counties relentlessly sought her out. Grace was a goldmine to our father, and giving her up to some mill worker was never going to be an option."

The touch on her hand applied more pressure, holding on as she made it through the retelling.

"It was at The Gathering. My father found Tommy and Grace in the library. That's why the mill workers are no longer allowed near Haven. He's forbidden their presence in our home ever since."

A sympathetic smile tugged at the corner of Noah's mouth. "And your sister and Tommy felt that they had no choice but to run away."

Grace would have run after that night whether Tommy had joined her or not. Once the guests departed from The Gathering, their father cornered Grace in her bedroom, locking them in while he taught her a lesson with his fists. The muffled screams that had come through the closed door still gave Willa nightmares, as did the scene when they were able to get inside. It had taken Cal to break down the door, but her father did not stop even then. He only halted his attack when Margaret and Bonnie rushed in, throwing themselves on top of Grace, who lay shaking on the floor.

Willa had stood helplessly in the doorway, holding a crying Lucy as they looked on in horror. The staff wisely stayed on the lower level, allowing the illustrious Fairweathers their moment to shine. The gossip would spread quickly and once Grace disappeared, no one ever blamed her for leaving.

"He beat Grace horribly that night, and she couldn't get out of bed for almost a week. Tommy became concerned after the first day, so he hid outside the house and even attempted to break in to get to Grace."

"I can't blame him. If it were you..." Noah pressed her flush to his chest. "I would have murdered him, Willa. I would have torn the walls of Haven House down to get to you."

Her cold hand warmed as it was released, their visitor's way of showing it was pleased with Noah's words. Yet, they only upset Willa. "You must never come for me. Ever. No matter if you think my life is in danger, do not come."

"Of course, I will come for you."

"No!"

She was getting upset, and the air suddenly felt much thinner than before. Her tears certainly weren't helping, but she couldn't stop. Instead of it being Tommy lying dead by the bayou, her mind showed her Noah. Lifeless. Drowned in a fit of rage.

"Grace got away. She got away, Noah. They were almost safe, but my father found them in the forest, right by the graveyard. We didn't know what was happening until it was too late."

It had been Cal who was alerted that something was off. Scheduled to go over the mill accounts, he sensed something was wrong when their father was late. Stephen Fairweather was never late for anything, and when a half hour passed, Cal took it upon himself to conduct a search. He'd gone upstairs first, and when he couldn't find any trace of their father, he went out onto the balcony to see if he was there. That was when he heard the screaming.

"My brother figured out something was wrong and came tearing through the house, shouting for help. We all made it out to the porch in time to see him bolt across the yard. I had never seen Cal run so fast."

Taking a steadying breath, she allowed herself a moment. Noah's concern was tearing at her soul, but she told herself she could be strong.

"We heard it then." She wiggled free of his hold on her but ended up bumping into a tree. With nowhere else to go, she remained plastered against its trunk as Noah and the ghost of her sister waited for her to speak. "Have you ever heard someone's heart breaking? It's awful and sounds as if the world truly is ending."

"Stay with me, love." Noah came over when she began to slide down the tree's trunk. "I've got you."

"We ran. Even me. We all ran as fast as we could toward Grace's screams, but it was too late. Tommy was dead. Drowned right there on the shore of the bayou near the graveyard." She was gasping, hardly able to speak as the memories returned to choke her. "Tommy had fought bravely for Grace, but he was no match for our father."

Noah held her up as the storm of emotions she'd kept bottled inside arrived in force. She cried against his chest, the clock ticking down on their time together.

"When we came upon them, Tommy was face down at the water's edge with Grace on her knees next to his body, pleading and crying for him to get up. There had been so much blood splattered about. On the ground, on the gravestones, everywhere."

The pain remained. It would be two years this Christmas, but the pain remained as strong as it did on the day it happened.

"We just stood there. Shocked and appalled. Bonnie was the first of us to snap out of it and went to my father, who was staring at his bruised hands. They were speaking, and we were listening, but none of us were watching." Her face scrunched tight. "None of us were watching Grace.

We didn't see her rise and march off to the mill. We didn't see as she… as she went straight to the point where the manchineel trees grow."

"Why would she go there?" Noah smoothed her hair from her face. "I know how poisonous manchineels are and how they can harm with just a touch. Your brother seems fascinated by them, and when I visited Beau several months ago, he kept hounding me over their venomous properties."

"Grace had gone there to enter the water, thinking no one would follow." Planted by her grandfather, the vile manchineels grew along the inlet point and served as a deterrent for the mill workers. Fairweathers never tolerated time wasted, even on hot days when an employee might want to take a dip in the cool water. "It was cold. I remember it was a cold day and close to Christmas, so the mill was closed. No one was around. No one was there to stop her from jumping into the water where the bayou meets the bay."

"She was trying to swim away?"

Willa did fall then, right to her knees. The tears streaming down her cheeks were just as worthless now as they were back then. "Grace couldn't swim. She was terrified of the water. We made it in time to see her disappear under the surface, and that was it. She was gone."

Even in the dark, she could see Noah's disbelief. "Your father? Your brother? None of you went in to save her?"

"We did."

A pointless endeavor, but they had tried. For their Grace, they had tried. Her father, bloody from his murderous fight with Tommy, screamed as he swam. Cal had used all his strength, diving right along with Bonnie when they came to where Grace had disappeared.

"Every one of us tried to reach her."

She didn't have the heart to tell him how she had run to the section of shore where there were no manchineel trees, terrified of their sap touching her skin. She didn't want him to know how she had only managed to make it waist-deep in the water before a breathing attack threatened. The shame of not being able to help her sister would chase her until the end of her days.

"My mother tried to save Grace, too," she whispered. "I told you she was different before, and she was. Before that day, she was light and happy whenever my father wasn't around. I was never a favorite, but I think she felt at least some sort of motherly emotion toward Lucy and me back then."

"Yet, she still seems to adore your brother?"

"Cal resembles Grace. Not only in looks but in personality. They're close in age and were as thick as thieves once upon a time." She took a deep inhale, the roar in her ears quieting. "When our mother looks at Lucy and me, all she sees are the disappointing daughters who remain, but Cal, he's the obedient son, always ready to give our mother whatever she wants."

Noah settled on the ground, placing his back against a tree. Pulling her into his lap, he wrapped them both in his long winter coat. "How has your family hidden this from everyone?"

She nearly laughed. He hadn't been around her family long enough to understand their ability to manipulate and deceive with ease. The famous Fairweather charm could move mountains with but a look.

However, when it came to Grace, they had been so very lost in their grief that day. The whole world had come crumbling down on them, and no one had known what to do.

"Bonnie," she replied. "Bonnie handled it."

Her father had continued to dive until he retrieved his eldest daughter's body, and once on shore, Cal had taken Grace from him, wrapping her in his coat as if he could keep her warm even in death. Her mother had wailed when they buried her firstborn in the graveyard. It had been an awful, keening cry of heartbreak, the likes of which Willa would never forget.

Willa rested her head on Noah's chest, allowing his erratic heartbeat to punch against her cheek. "Bonnie returned to the house first and whispered to the staff that Grace and Tommy had slipped off through the bayou to run away, and we had tried to stop them. It explained why we were wet and distraught."

"And what about Tommy?" His chin rubbed along the top of her head as if he were thinking this all through. "What happened to his body?"

"We buried him with Grace."

Her father had fought against it, but when Margaret Fairweather's mind snapped, he'd had no choice but to comply. To this day, Willa truly believed that if he hadn't agreed, her mother would have had Cal kill her husband right there on the spot.

"When we went back to the house, none of the staff questioned us. They only clucked their tongues as if to say what a shame, but behind our backs, they whispered how happy they were for Grace."

Noah's lips pressed to her temple, and the dark void watching fled, having seen and heard enough. Willa nearly began crying again, hoping beyond hope that Grace was simply returning to her Tommy. That they had found each other somehow.

"They'll whisper the same things about you," Noah said softly. "They'll say good for Willa. Running off to marry the man she loves. A man that's going to give her the world."

She lifted her head, meeting his steely gaze. "Are you?"

"I am." Noah helped her stand, his outrage a mixture of fury and remorse. She understood the fury, but the remorse embedded itself in her brain. He was fighting the urge to sweep her away right then and was feeling guilty because he knew it just wasn't possible yet. "But first, I have to get you out of that house."

CHAPTER 16

H e asked her to give him three days. "Don't expect me to come for my usual visits, as I don't want to raise suspicion."

"Why would you raise suspicion if you visited me?"

Noah had smiled at the question. "Because you're mine now, and every one of them will realize it the second they see us together."

She'd lifted her chin, a little perturbed at him for insinuating that she couldn't pull off a ruse. "I can behave."

With a rough squeeze on her bottom and a final kiss that left her weak in the knees, Noah shook his head. "I can't."

When they parted, he planned to write to Dr. Parsons in Ohio and to his parents, but he didn't want to tell his brother yet. "I love Beau, but he's never been able to lie a single day in his life. I'll leave him a note, and he can be our eyes and ears here once we're gone."

Their plan for departure was to take place on the third night, directly at midnight. He would signal by lantern again, and they would ride off on Hope and enter a new life.

It would work. Willa had to believe it would work and trusted Noah completely. However, as it turned out, while Noah had thought his presence would cause suspicion, his absence did the same.

Alone in the library the next day, she didn't notice Bonnie staring from the doorway at first. "And where is Dr. Anderson this afternoon?"

Head down and eyes on the book she was reading, Willa replied evenly, "I'm not sure."

She sat curled on the couch, having chosen the library rather than her usual lounger in the conservatory for two reasons. The first being that she thought she might hide her small suitcase in the conservatory and didn't want to draw attention to the spot.

The second was that the library's couch had more cushioning than the one in the conservatory, and when she had awakened with an ache leftover from her night with Noah, Willa had taken great care not to alert anyone to her tender state.

She couldn't very well walk around wincing all day.

"It's Tuesday." Bonnie stepped into the room, a furry army of cats accompanying her. The beasts spread throughout the room as they slinked in, taking up space on various pieces of furniture. "He always comes on Tuesdays."

Lucy passed the door, humming a jaunty Christmas tune. "It is the holiday season," Willa said, closing her book. "Perhaps he's busy with family affairs."

Hearing her speak, Lucy spun into the room. "Willa, you have a note!"

It was probably another letter from Mr. Richards. He wrote three times a day, and while Willa never bothered to read them since Lucy had completely taken over corresponding with him, she held out a hand for the envelope. "Mr. Richards?"

Lucy shook her head. "It's from Dr. Anderson."

Heat crept up her neck, a flush she couldn't stop as she stood from the couch to take the letter. She missed him to a degree she hadn't thought possible.

"Let me have it." Bonnie snatched the note before Willa's fingers could connect with the paper. "What does the dear doctor have to say that he cannot say in person?"

Bile shot into Willa's throat. "I beg your pardon, but that letter is addressed to me."

Ignoring her, Bonnie read the entire thing in seconds. "It appears he has a cold." Her dark gaze lifted to connect with Willa's. "As a doctor, one would think he would know that traipsing around in the woods so late at night can cause these types of ailments."

Beneath Willa's feet, it felt as if the floor had crumbled away, leaving nothing but the fiery pits of hell to lick at her heels. "What do you mean?"

Bonnie stuffed the letter into the pocket of her apron. "Lucy, leave us."

Too wrapped up in reading another letter, her sister giggled at whatever was on the page and left without so much as a backward glance.

A tightness squeezed Willa's chest, and she attempted to remain calm. One word from Bonnie to her father, and she would need all her faculties to deal with his wrath.

"Your sister is growing close with John Richards." Bonnie went to the library door and closed it with a soft click. "I'm assuming you've noticed?"

Sinking slowly, Willa sat perched on the edge of the couch. "I have."

"And you are not bothered by this?"

"I'm supposed to marry him," Willa began. "Wanting my sister to get along wi—"

Bonnie cut her off with a cluck of the tongue. "I know about Paul and that Katie girl."

Staff gossiped—it was the way of things—but Bonnie knowing Paul Anderson's secret was a bit of a surprise. Most of the staff at Haven House never regarded her as one of them.

"News from the Anderson's household?"

Sitting next to her, Bonnie heaved out a sigh. "It's not pretty over there. Ulrich is furious, but Paul is adamant that he loves Katie."

"I noticed Katie is not here anymore." None of the Port Michaelson girls were. Not even Jennie was loitering about this afternoon. "Did you dismiss them?"

"From my understanding, they know to stay away now that Katie has ruined their fun. If your father were to be made aware of what Cal and the rest of you have been up to…"

She didn't need to finish. They all knew there would be hell to pay.

"I only recently became aware of Cal courting Jennie," Willa replied. "I know it's a sore subject, but perhaps he will understand the attachment because of you."

In the corner, a cat hissed, its hackles rising at the remark.

"Sore subject?" Bonnie raised her own hackles, her dark hazel eyes glazing over with a fiery anger she rarely let show. "If anyone is sore in this room, it is you, Wilhelmina. Care to explain what went on last night?"

Willa counted the seconds, keeping the steady metronome of air flowing. The technique, which she learned at a young age, helped her keep an attack at bay when upset.

And it wouldn't help to lie. Bonnie never made accusations without proof.

"Cal told you?"

The color in Bonnie's cheeks dimmed, fleeing as she paled. "Your brother knows?"

"He was out on the porch with Jennie around midnight," Willa confessed. The truth might as well come out now, so when she went missing in two days, someone would have a vague idea of where she had gone. "I don't know what they were doing."

"Oh, I'm sure I can guess," Bonnie said sarcastically.

Willa blinked at her. Could she? Could this tiny woman who always held herself to the highest level of decorum truly understand what it meant to engage in such things?

As if reading her mind, Bonnie chuckled and checked to ensure the library door was securely closed. "Yes, Willa. Your father had me several times over before marrying your mother."

Willa's mouth opened and closed, her brain not knowing quite what words to release. The image...no. She would not allow her mind to show her the sight.

"Oh."

The lackluster response had Bonnie grinning widely, and the sight of her smile struck Willa into silence. It was easy to forget how beautiful this woman could be when she was happy. Much like her own mother, when the veil of harshness and pain brought on by Stephen Fairweather was lifted, the two women positively glowed.

"He's not a good man. Never has been. Yet, strangely, I think that's what drew me to him. Stephen was awful to everyone but me, and I fell right into love with him because of it." The smile drifted downward, losing its momentum. "And he loved me right back, but we both understood that for all this to survive—for us to survive—sacrifices had to be made."

"What are you trying to say?"

"Cal is not serious about this dalliance with Jennie. He knows he has a responsibility to marry well, just as his father did."

A weight the size of an elephant sat in her stomach, and Willa turned away. "Just as I do."

"Not necessarily." Bonnie laid a hand on Willa's leg. "Paul Anderson is no longer an option for your sister."

"Ulrich can change his mind and force the match, especially once Father hears of what has happened."

"Katie is with child."

Willa's head snapped back around. "You're joking."

Smug as ever, Bonnie nodded. "As I said, Paul Anderson is no longer an option for Lucy, but Mr. Richards is. We need that land, and just as what's grown between you and Dr. Anderson, your sister and John are engaging in something more than a simple attachment."

Willa didn't know what to say, not sure if this was a trick, but then Bonnie snatched her hand. "Listen to me," Bonnie whispered. "I don't want to know what you have planned."

"I don't have anything planned," Willa lied.

With a roll of her eyes, Bonnie sighed. "I have known you since you entered this world, Wilhelmina, and I can tell that you and your doctor have something planned." She waved a hand in the air, flapping it in frustration. "But that doesn't matter. I don't want to know the details."

"Alright."

It was all the confirmation Bonnie needed, and she hugged Willa, who went stiff in her arms. The sensation of being held felt strange. No one in this house ever touched her in such a manner.

"That's my girl. I knew you were strong," Bonnie murmured, cupping the back of Willa's head. "From here on out, you must ignore what you hear or see, and when it comes time to follow through with your plans, you will go. Don't look back, just go."

Up in her room, Willa dressed for dinner. Every night until the new year, her father would demand that they present themselves in formal attire during their evening meal as if Haven House were entertaining the masses when really it was only the Fairweathers and Bonnie around the table.

Her odd discussion with Bonnie the day prior had ended abruptly when her mother swept into the library. "What's going on in here?" Margaret had flung open the library door, sending the cats scattering. "What are you two discussing?"

"Willa was feeling a little ill," Bonnie had informed her. "I didn't want to upset anyone else, so we shut ourselves up in the library until it passed."

The excuse had been enough for her mother, who sent Willa out so she could discuss the Christmas schedule for the following week with Bonnie. Willa had to give it to them. Haven was looking beyond lovely, with decorations and reminders of the season stuffed into every corner.

Bonnie never approached her again, and too terrified over her plans, Willa kept to her room. The time alone had given her a chance to think. She had so many questions. How far would they travel that first day? They needed to get to a rail depot, but the closest one was nearly fifty miles from Haven House. Would they take the horse the whole way? Could she ride for that long? What if she had an attack while they traveled?

The leaves for the tea Noah claimed would help ease her lung spasms were stored safely in her top dresser drawer, and she would be sure to bring them, but it wasn't as if she could put a kettle on while traveling by horse.

However, even with all these unanswered questions, she had complete faith in Noah. He would never fail her. Never. She was solid in the belief that his intentions were true and his love for her was real.

As she fixed her hair in the mirror, a commotion in the hallway caught her attention. Concerned over what might be happening, she slowly approached her bedroom door but fell back in shock when the thing burst open and her father stormed in.

"What have you done?"

He wasn't shouting, though the deadly quiet rage coming off him was enough to send Willa scrambling as he stalked her across the room. "Nothing."

"Lies," he hissed. "You are a lying whore."

"I didn't do anything."

The back of his hand struck her cheek, and Willa stumbled, unable to catch herself before falling to the hard floor. Landing on her side, she wheezed, the wind knocked out of her from the impact.

"What did you say to John Richards?"

She scurried like an injured animal into the room's corner. The hit on her face burned, and the pain radiating from her right hip and arm didn't permit her to move very fast. "Nothing!" The word came out on a wheeze, the familiar tightness inflaming her chest. She needed to lower her voice and work on breathing. "I have not spoken to John Richards."

Standing above her, Stephen Fairweather coldly stared at his daughter trembling on the floor. "But you write to him?"

"No."

"Do not lie to me, Wilhelmina."

"I don't write to him. I never have." Like a coward, she held her cheek and sobbed. "Lucy has been sending him the letters, not me."

"Are you telling me that it is your little sister who is owed my wrath?"

Curling into herself, Willa tucked into a ball. She hated him. *Hated.* There was not one redeeming quality about this man. He was no father. The mill was his offspring—his only love—and not even a hopelessly devoted Bonnie could pierce the heart of Stephen Fairweather. "Don't you dare hurt Lucy."

"John Richards has withdrawn his pursuit of you. A letter arrived today, expressing his stance and how he felt as though you were never truly invested in a courtship with him."

A stampede of footsteps carried up the stairs. On the floor and behind her bed, Willa couldn't see who had arrived, but she called out to them anyway.

"What's this?" Bonnie rushed around the bed and stopped short when she saw Willa. "Stephen?"

"Richards has decided that he and Wilhelmina are not a good match."

"And you punish Willa for the man's poor judgment?" Bending down, Bonnie wrapped an arm around Willa's lower back to support her in sitting upright. "That's not exactly fair, is it?"

Margaret appeared, and she watched Willa with the same grotesque detachment as her husband. "What isn't fair is that we needed that land," she said. "The mill requires it to survive."

Helping Willa stand, Bonnie shook her head. "But if the Andersons and Fairweathers merge, we might not need the Hollingsdale property."

"You have no say in the matter," Margaret snapped at Bonnie. "Now, go downstairs and see if Mrs. Graham will have dinner prepared on time."

The dismissal shocked everyone in the room. The kinship between Bonnie and her mother was unmatched, and to hear Margaret order her friend about in such a way was odd. Willa was sure her father would turn his fury on his wife.

But he didn't, and when Bonnie made no move to leave, it was Stephen who jerked his head toward the door. "Go on, Bon."

Reluctantly, Bonnie released her, and Willa nearly toppled over again. She tried to walk to the corner chair but didn't quite make it, holding on to its back as she strained for air. A coughing fit was on the rise, and a coughing fit only meant a severe attack was imminent.

"Get ahold of yourself." Her father had no patience when it came to her illness. "You're not getting out of this conversation, Wilhelmenia. I don't care if you can breathe or not."

She shook her head, the strands of her hair sticking to her wet cheeks. There was no getting ahold of herself. The attack was in its beginning stage, building into a crescendo that would leave her vulnerable.

"Noah." Hissing his name like a prayer, she begged her parents. "Please. I need help."

"That man is never coming here again." Her father crossed his arms. "He fills your head with nonsense and is likely the entire cause of Richards backing off."

"Or Richards has turned from one Fairweather to another," Bonnie said. She hadn't left, standing directly behind Willa while wisely not offering her assistance. "What did the letter say exactly, Stephen?"

From his pocket, Willa watched through her spotty vision as her father produced a piece of paper and handed it to Bonnie, who skimmed the missive quickly. "Where's the rest?" She flipped to the back and saw that it was blank. "There was more, wasn't there?"

Willa didn't bother to try to make out the words as she could hardly follow what was happening when her mother rushed over to read the letter with Bonnie.

"Stephen?" Margaret snatched the letter from Bonnie. "This note is only one page and ends in the middle of a sentence. What did you do with the second page?"

"Richards is an imbecile at best," he grumbled. "The fool likely forgot to place the rest of the letter in the envelope."

"John is not a fool," Lucy said from the doorway, and all heads spun in her direction. "He's quite brilliant."

"Get out, Lucy," their father ordered. "I plan to deal with you later."

Braver than all of them, Lucy stuck her chin in the air. "What did the rest of the letter say?" she persisted. "Was it about me?"

"None of it matters." Marching across the room, Stephen Fairweather seized his youngest child by the upper arm and shook her. "You are to marry Paul Anderson."

Willa pushed her way to the chair, knocking Bonnie and her mother aside. "Please help me." She waved a frantic hand at the dresser across the room where she had hidden the tea leaves. "Leaves for a tea." Her finger shook as she pointed to the drawer. "Treatment from Noah."

No one paid her any attention.

"Paul is marrying a young woman named Katie," Bonnie announced, placing a hand on Margaret's arm. "You'll remember her, Stephen. She was the pretty blonde girl we hired to work in the kitchens."

Lucy's face turned a disturbing shade of pale while their father's went blistering red. "Ulrich will never stand for it. Paul is promised to Lucy, and the mills will merge. He would never throw his entire fortune away on the whims of that no-good son."

"And yet, he is." Bonnie went to the dresser drawer where Willa was pointing and retrieved the small bag of leaves. "Lucy, your sister needs help. Take this downstairs and instruct Mrs. Graham to make tea with it. Once it's ready, bring a cup immediately."

Finally realizing Willa's distress, Lucy rushed over. "Yes, of course."

"Be quick about it," Bonnie said, handing her the bag. "Shut the door on your way out."

Knowing not to argue, Lucy hurried from the room, closing the door as she went.

"The girl is pregnant, Stephen." Bonnie returned to the corner, bypassing Margaret to take Willa's hand. "It's confirmed."

Margaret at least had the decency to gasp. "You must be joking. With a kitchen maid?"

The insult wasn't lost on Bonnie, and she flinched. "Paul is said to be elated, and the couple will marry at Christmas."

"Paul Anderson can't marry some kitchen maid," her father bellowed loud enough that Willa swore she felt the bones of Haven House quake in fear. If her heart hadn't already been racing, it would have jolted in sheer terror at his barely contained anger. "In order to survive, sacrifices must be made."

"Times are different," Bonnie replied calmly. "The world is changing."

"The world will never change enough to where a man who is set to inherit can marry the woman he wants."

Bitterness clung to every word, his own destiny serving as a reminder of how things *should* be done.

"What's happening here?" Cal stumbled into the room red-faced and chest pumping. He looked as if he'd run a mile to get there. "Willa?"

"She's having an attack, Cal." Margaret moved around the bed to keep her son back, pushing his chest lightly. "Go downstairs."

Cal refused to budge, staring menacingly at their father. "What have you done to her?"

"None of your business, boy," their father spat out. "But if I hear that you knew anything about Paul Anderson and that kitchen maid, it'll be you next."

Something behind Cal's eyes snapped, and their mother was shoved aside. "And how exactly will you deal with me?"

Willa felt her gut clench in dreaded anticipation. Her brother rarely allowed his temper free anymore. Not like he did when he was younger.

Not since he'd become a grown man who grasped the importance of tucking away that Fairweather darkness in favor of being charming.

Their mother was in front of Cal again. Hands on his shoulders, she desperately whispered for him to remain calm. Willa couldn't hear exactly what was being said, but whatever it was did the trick. Cal listened and met their mother's gaze with a curt nod, the storm of his anger passing before it ever had a chance to descend upon them.

"Cal and I are going to hurry them along with Willa's tea, but if it doesn't work, we're sending for the doctor, no matter what you say," Margaret said over her shoulder as she led Cal to the door. "We don't need yet another dead daughter in this family."

With her mother gone, Bonnie helped Willa onto the bed. "Paul's woman is pregnant, Stephen. You cannot change that fact."

"There are ways," he came over to sneer at Willa as if he were watching a half dead dog dying in the streets. "We both know there are ways, and that damn doctor over there can help."

Willa stiffened at the mention of Noah, which was a mistake. The strain on her muscles caused a coughing fit to take hold, and with her insides on fire, she clawed at the bedspread, trying to brace herself as the attack mounted its strength.

"Don't you remember how excited we were?" Bonnie rubbed circles on Willa's back, massaging gently until the fit eased. "Remember how big our dreams had been at that age?"

"We were fools, Bon. So blindly happy we didn't see how it would fail us in the end." Her father scrubbed a hand down his face. "Destiny smiled down upon us for a single day and then stole it away before we could love her."

"Oh, now I don't believe that," Bonnie replied, soft and kind. "We loved her, and she knew we loved her. How could she not? I've never in my life seen you as happy as you were when you held her for the first time."

"Ah, Bon. You shouldn't hold on so tight to her memory."

"Why not? It's all I have." Bonnie's mouth screwed tight. "And you think I blame you when I don't. No one is to blame, just as no one is to blame for Willa having the same breathing affliction as our baby girl. I'm sorry you were the one holding her when it happened, Stephen. I'm sorry I fell asleep, and you were the only one with her when she passed."

"Don't do it to yourself, Bon," her father said gruffly. "There's no point in living in the past."

"You think about her as much as I do," Bonnie insisted. "Deny it all you want, but I see the flowers you leave on her little grave."

Rolling to her side, Willa's hazy mind tried to follow what they were saying, but it didn't make sense. Who were they talking about, and what little grave?

"She deserves to be remembered as much as Gracie," her father murmured. "Our girl would have outshined every one of them if she had lived."

If she had lived.

It came to Willa all at once. In the rear corner of the graveyard, a small, unmarked stone lay half-buried in the dirt. A child's grave, which she assumed was some long-lost relative from the past. She only knew it was there because whenever she worked up the courage to visit Grace, there would be little sprigs of flowers on the marker from time to time.

Her father had left the flowers.

Her father and Bonnie had once had a child together.

"But it was for the best that she didn't."

Bonnie stilled at his cruel words, holding her breath as she listened.

"There was no place for her in this world, Bon," her father continued. "No place for her as a Fairweather."

Closing her eyes, Bonnie nodded and turned her head when a tear rolled down her cheek. She quickly wiped it away and regained her composure within seconds of it falling. "Let Lucy be happy. Give her to Richards. The marriage will secure the planting land in Hollingsdale," she told him, stroking Willa's hair. "We have another in with the Anderson family, and if an alliance forms, the mills will grow, securing that the Fairweathers will always remain at Haven House, as it should be."

"You can't mean Wilhelmina?" Her father's dark eyes squinted at her wheezing on the bed. "The doctor might be entertaining himself with a little flirtation, but he's too handsome. He'll leave this place and forget all about her."

Bonnie chuckled. "He's already had her, Stephen. The deed is done, and she could be with child already."

Moaning in denial, Willa braced for her father's anger, knowing in this state she would not survive if he chose to physically attack.

"Well, well, Willa. Aren't you a surprise?" Her father kneeled to look her dead in the face. "I would have never thought you'd have the courage to do something like that."

"They used his medical cottage from what the whispers are saying, and I was quite tickled by the irony." Bonnie turned to speak directly to Willa. "That's where your father and I would go in our younger years. It was our little 'house' where we pretended the world was different and we could be together," she said. "Our daughter was even born there. On a cold January morning, she took her first breath, and by the afternoon, she took her last."

Willa didn't know if she should be shocked or horrified or both, but it was the one time in her life when she was thankful for this awful disorder's ability to rob her of speech.

"We won't get anything out of the Andersons if she's dead. Where is that damn tea?" Her father rose to stand and turned to the door as if he were expecting someone to magically appear. "Or perhaps we should call the doctor?"

Bonnie watched him pacing, her gaze shifting into a quiet resolve as she tracked his movements. "That bruise on her cheek will just upset him. It's best to leave calling Dr. Anderson over as a last resort."

Groaning between the hacking, Willa could only listen to Bonnie's reasoning even though she wanted to cry out in denial. She needed Noah. This attack could be one of her worst, and she was terrified.

Her father grunted something under his breath and returned to examine her. "Do you really think Noah Anderson is going to make a wife out of Willa?" he asked, a bit perplexed. "Willa? Bon, be serious. How on earth is *she* ever going to make him happy?"

"Have a little faith." Bonnie patted Willa's hip, the very one she had landed on. It hurt like the devil, and she had a feeling Bonnie knew it. "We can help her. Margaret and I can teach her how to please a man properly."

Willa covered her face with her hands. This sickeningly bizarre conversation bordered on the insane and was causing her chest to hurt as much as her head.

"You be the one to talk to her, Bon. That wife of mine couldn't please a dead man," her father's gruff voice said. "And you listen to me, girl. If you can secure yourself an Anderson that will force Ulrich to merge our mills, then I'll throw you the biggest damn wedding in the history of Haven House."

CHAPTER 17

I'll throw you the biggest damn wedding in the history of Haven House.

Lying flat on her back, Willa watched the shadows dance on the ceiling. Everything hurt. Every bone in her body held an aching weariness like she hadn't felt in years.

Throw her a wedding? Was he joking?

She had almost laughed. Lost in her attack, she had truly almost laughed directly in his horrible face. All she had ever wanted was for them to accept her. They never had to love her. Hoping for a Fairweather to love something other than themselves was a stretch, but accepting her? Had that been too much to ask?

And now, in the blink of an eye, when she was suddenly a useful pawn, he wanted to give her a beautiful wedding. The years of abuse ran deep in this house, and he wasn't about to erase them with a pretty party to celebrate the daughter he could hardly tolerate.

Stifling a groan so as not to wake anyone, Willa rose from the bed. She only had one more night here. One more day to make it through. Looking around her room, she felt suddenly nostalgic, reliving all the memories the space held. The conservatory was her public sanctuary, but here in her room, she could pretend to be anything she wanted.

In her younger years, it had been her and Grace. Playing for hours while Willa was always inevitably ill, she and her sister created kingdoms from their imagination. Cal would join in every so often, forced to participate as the diabolical villain. When Lucy came along, it had been such fun to show their smallest sibling the tiny world they had created right under Haven's roof.

But then time moved on. Bored with their games, her brother and sisters left her, each seeking to discover the real world—to have real adventures—without her.

Grimacing at the pain radiating from her shoulder, Willa tried to stretch the muscle. She should sleep. It was desperately needed, but she was too nervous over the possibilities of tomorrow, and as her brain rehashed every question a thousand times over, one singular thought was louder than the rest.

Would she be enough?

Would Noah truly love her forever? Would he willingly grow old with her? Would she be enough to keep a man like him captivated for all eternity?

Or was her father right? Would Noah grow tired of her eventually?

Self-doubt was almost as devious a demon as hope. The two emotions warred inside her brain, making her feel foolish and unsure of everything.

What if they left, and he abandoned her on the way to Ohio? But what if they settled down and lived happily ever after? What if his parents hated her? But what if his parents loved her? What if her condition grew worse, and he found himself tied to a person he was required to tend to night and day? But what if she got better up north and could live like a normal person?

Covering her mouth, Willa attempted to cease her crying, but it was impossible. Being shunned her entire life and treated as if she was less of a person because of her illness had taken its toll. The neglect had destroyed the woman she might have been. A woman who might have easily enthralled Noah Anderson and kept him happy.

Perhaps she should stay. They would marry and live close, with him opening a medical practice and her figuring out how to function as a wife. Haven House could continue to serve as her refuge should Noah one day realize she wasn't worth the effort.

Yes, that was it. That was the perfect idea. She would give her father exactly what he wanted and—*Grace's song.*

As it had been, the melody grew, giving Willa no choice but to follow. Stepping out onto the balcony, she breathed in the crisp night air. It would be a lovely Yule season here at Haven House, and while she never had much joy living under its roof, she did love the illusion of happiness the holiday season brought to her home.

The haunting song grew, floating on the evening breeze as it encircled where she stood. Leaning on the balcony, Willa closed her eyes and aimed her face toward the singing voice.

"Should I stay, Grace?" she whispered, thinking herself a lunatic. "Should Noah and I make our home here? Father is happy, and Mother will be as well, I assume. The marriage will give them the alliance and... I love him, Grace. You know I love him."

She felt it. So very sure what was happening was real, she leaned into the caress against her cheek. Willa was positive Noah felt Grace's presence with them in the forest, but in the light of day, would he believe? Or would this be just another quirk of hers that might eventually drive him away?

"I love him, Grace, but what if I'm not enough?" She didn't hide her tears, not with her sister's comforting touch here. "I'm so very broken, and I don't understand how he can want me. Should I stay in case he one day doesn't want me?"

The song halted, and a single word replaced the melody.

Go.

Go.

Grace was telling her to go. *Run.* Willa could feel the rush, the absolute need to place as much possible distance between herself and Haven

House. The urgency to flee mixed with her desire for Noah, and once her eyes snapped open, the decision was made.

"I'll go," Willa whispered to the dark swirling shadows weaving their return to the forest. "I'll go and never look back."

CHAPTER 18

The following day passed without incident. Willa emerged from her room around mid-morning, having breakfast alone in the conservatory as always. Bonnie checked on her in the afternoon, inquiring if she was prepared for her reading of *A Christmas Carol*.

Willa understood Bonnie was only attempting to make small talk and indulged her. It was her way of glossing over what had occurred the day before. Anytime her father's temper took on a rage-fueled life of its own, the aftermath was nothing but pleasantries and false cheer.

"Yes, I'm ready for my reading," Willa replied.

Producing the best smile she could muster, Bonnie nodded. "Good thing. Christmas Eve is right around the corner."

Having nothing else to add, Bonnie and her usual herd of cats departed, leaving Willa to her own devices throughout the day.

And then it was her mother's turn. Close to sunset, Margaret whisked into the conservatory to say her peace. "I've been told you are to marry."

Straightening on the chaise lounge, Willa met her mother's cold stare. "Yes, ma'am."

Margaret sniffed the air, looking anywhere but at her daughter. "Your father is speaking with Ulrich about it all tomorrow."

Tomorrow?

Tomorrow, she would be gone.

"That sounds wonderful."

As if it was a struggle, Margaret's gaze finally landed on her. "He is quite handsome. Let us hope you do not muck it up."

Lifting her chin, Willa matched her mother's obstinate tone. "Yes, let us hope."

Having heard enough, Margaret left her, and not long after, Lucy snuck in for a chat. While she would not miss the others, Willa would sorely miss her sister.

"Come sit with me, Lucy."

They snuggled together on the chaise, holding each other on the lower level where no one could see them. "We're going to be wives, Willa," Lucy whispered. "John has asked for my hand!"

"Oh, Lucy!" Willa whispered back. "I am so happy for you, but you must promise me something."

Hearing the hitch in her voice, Lucy lifted her head from Willa's shoulder. "What?"

"That you'll marry John quickly," she replied. "Don't prolong the engagement. Go. Leave Haven and start your life right away."

Lucy grinned. "I plan to."

Everyone ignored them as they had their evening meal together in the conservatory. Night descended as they ate, with the stars and moon overtaking the burnt sunset sky.

Lucy held up her glass of wine. "This is our victory dinner, Willa."
Our last one.

Taking her own glass, Willa clinked it against Lucy's goblet. "To us."

Lucy snorted out a giggle, having had too much wine already. "To us."

They went to bed without seeing a soul. Even the household and kitchen staff seemed to have gone to bed by the time they finished.

"Goodness, it's barely eight o'clock," Lucy noted as they put their plates in the kitchen. "Is everyone asleep already?"

It was odd but would work out well for her plans, and Willa chalked the turn of events to the universe granting her a bit of luck for once. "I suppose so."

Going upstairs, Willa couldn't help but hug Lucy before saying goodnight. "I love you, Lucy."

Would this be the last time she saw her sister? Perhaps, but John Richards was a good man who would take care of his wife.

"I love you, too, Willow."

The smile on Willa's face disappeared, and she pulled back to look her little sister over. No one called her Willow.

No one except Grace.

"Why…" Willa's eyes searched Lucy's face. "Why would you call me that?"

Lucy shrugged. "I dreamed about Grace the other night, and her old nickname for you has been in my head for days now."

Pressing her lips together, Willa gave her a tight smile. "How unusual."

"She said the same thing in my dream as you did earlier," Lucy said, wobbly on her feet as she headed for her bedroom door. "I'm to marry John Richards quickly and start my life far, far away from Haven House."

Willa said goodnight and entered her bedroom, but instead of settling between the sheets to sleep, she gathered the hidden satchel and changed into her traveling attire. A long coat, loose skirt, and a pair of riding trousers she'd had to steal from Lucy.

As midnight approached, she took one last look at her room and went to the window to wait for Noah's signal. As expected, a tiny flare of light flashed from the edge of trees at the front of the house when the clock struck twelve.

Leaving her room, she waited on the landing to listen for movement, and hearing none, made her way silently downstairs.

No one was stirring, not even a mouse.

On the ground floor, her erratic heartbeat faltered for but a moment. Willa had made peace with never seeing her conservatory again, but on the way to the foyer, she spared the library a brief glance. Perhaps in the future, this place might be filled with Fairweathers who loved reading as much as she did.

Making it to the foyer, she clasped her satchel tightly and turned to say goodbye to Haven House. The massive hallway expanded outward, the grandfather clock ticking away at the seconds of her final moments. It truly was a beautiful place, and if ever loved properly, would become something special.

"Goodbye, old girl," Willa whispered as she took in all the splendor of Christmas staring back at her. It was fitting to be saying goodbye during the time of year when Haven was at her most beautiful. "May you one day know peace."

And with that, Wilhelmina Fairweather departed Haven House for the last time.

CHAPTER 19

"I almost thought you weren't coming." Noah kissed her like they had been apart for years and not mere days. "You took forever."

"I'm sorry, but this is the first time I've ever been whisked off to a new life, Noah Anderson," she teased, beyond happy to be in his arms again. "Forgive me for not knowing I should rush."

With a growl, his tongue coaxed past her lips, sweeping in to claim what was already his to take. "I'm half tempted to stop by the cottage before we depart and teach you the importance of being prompt."

"Well, maybe you should."

He nipped at her bottom lip. "Tempting, but I don't want you sore for the ride."

The moon overhead chose that moment to peek out from behind the clouds and shine directly on them. Noah's excitement faded swiftly when he saw the bruise on her cheek, his expression slowly—painfully—morphing into absolute rage.

Holding her chin, he examined the mark. "Who did this?"

"So, much has happened."

She told him everything, and with each sentence, his anger deepened. "He struck you, *and* you had an attack, and they still did not call for me?"

"It wasn't a bad one." Conditioned to defend them, Willa tried to shrug off his concern. "The tea worked, and I made sure to rest today and not do anything too strenuous, so I was prepared for tonight."

"If I ever see him again, I'll kill him, Willa." Noah's thumb stroked the underside of the bruise. "I'm half tempted to go into that God-forsaken house and do the deed now. The world would be a better place for it."

"No, you will not. We're leaving and will never think of him again." Taking his wrist with two hands, she halted the caress against her cheek. "Let your family's mill merge with ours. Let them have their win because it doesn't matter. I'm free. I'm yours."

His lips claimed hers, the desperation and rage merging with desire. "You *are* mine, and I will spend the rest of my life proving it."

"Promise?"

The single word was all she could muster, and the two of them separated to grin wildly in the dark.

"Promise," he replied with one final kiss on the tip of her nose. "It's time to go."

Taking the satchel from her, he held her hand and led them down the lane to where Hope waited at its end. From all around, Haven's nighttime chorus of birds and vermin chittered about as they walked. The evening breeze shaking the trees and moss overhead in a noisy farewell.

"It's a shame," Noah observed. "This place is lovely, albeit remote."

Willa smiled. "When I left, I was thinking that maybe Haven would one day know peace."

"I'm sure she wil—"

A crack echoed through the night. Sharp and final, it silenced the world and had Noah shoving her behind him.

"What was that?" Willa whispered, sandwiched between the base of a pine tree and Noah's massive back. "It sounded like a gun—"

A series of shouts carried over on the wind, and Noah pressed her further against the tree. "It's coming from the mill."

The extensive side and rear yards could be seen from their position on the lane. It was a wide, open space with a handful of trees spread around the main central oak standing guard over the estate. And at the end of it all, where the thick pelt of green grass ended at the bayou, a line of pine served as the barrier between Haven and the mill's land.

Noah squinted at a figure emerging from the house. "Where the devil is she going?"

Looking over his shoulder, Willa could make out a lone figure walking across the lawn. "Is that Bonnie?"

Bundled in her dressing gown and robe, complete with her usual nighttime hair wrappings, Bonnie strode across the lawn at an even pace.

Not but a second later, Willa's mother appeared, exiting from Haven's rear kitchen door just as Bonnie had. The pair headed toward the forest trails where the narrow paths led out to the inlet point and the mill, passing their family graveyard on the way.

They waited a moment, and when nothing else happened, Willa tugged on Noah's shirt. "Let's go."

Another shot rang out.

"Hell." Noah spun around and gave her a quick kiss before preparing to dart across the lawn. "Stay here."

"Absolutely not!" Willa chased after him, cutting across the thick green grass. "You are not about to run off in the direction of gunshots and expect me to stay behind."

He didn't argue and took her hand as they sprinted to the forest. Upon entering the dense woodland canopy, Willa shrunk behind Noah when she immediately noticed the unnatural quiet. There were no animals—no noise—almost as if the forest were as frightened as she was.

"This isn't right," she said, clutching his hand tightly. "Something is very wrong here, Noah."

He signaled for her to be quiet with a finger to his lips, and they kept to the side of the trail, making sure to stay well hidden among the trees. The deeper they went, the more the silence grew until they reached the sharp bend leading directly into the graveyard.

Stopping behind Noah, she tried to make out the soft rumble of voices ahead. "Whoever is out there is in the graveyard," Willa whispered. "I can see movement but can't make out how many."

"I hear your brother." Noah turned and grabbed her upper arms, moving her further into the brush. "Don't leave this spot. I'm going to sneak along the water's edge and try to make out what is happening."

"I will do no such thing." She shook her head furiously. "You either take me, or we turn around and leave."

Noah swiped a hand through his hair. "Are you always going to be this stubborn?"

"Yes, she is." From behind Noah, a figure emerged from the shadows. "And now that you're getting a taste of our Willa's true nature, I hope you're not having second thoughts on marrying her, Dr. Anderson."

Bonnie.

Holding a gun.

A gun aimed at Noah's face when he spun around.

Immediately, Willa was in front of the man she loved, blocking him from harm. Bonnie didn't scare her. The woman had practically raised her.

"What are you doing?"

"Why didn't you just go, Willa?" Bonnie sighed but kept the gun level. "I swear sometimes you're no better than my cats. You're always so curious until a tail gets cut right off."

Perhaps she should be afraid. The look in Bonnie's eyes held a hint of madness in them. Noah must have noticed, too, because she was quickly shoved behind him again. "We'll leave."

"Oh, I'm afraid it's too late for that, but this turn of events is a good thing. You see, we've come to an impasse and need assistance." The gun wagged in the direction of the graveyard. "Walk ahead, please."

Noah debated, assessing how much of a threat Bonnie was to them. "And if I don't?"

"Then we'll have three bodies to bury instead of just the two."

CHAPTER 20

"Not that I think you can't do it, Willa." Bonnie kept the gun trained on the back of Noah's head, smiling wistfully as she made the remark. "But you're going to have to work extra hard to keep a man like him satisfied."

With her head held high and spine straight, Willa wanted to scream as she was forced to walk arm-in-arm with Bonnie. Noah remained a few steps ahead on the forest path, glancing back every so often to check on her.

There were more people in the graveyard, and when they neared the curve, Willa half expected to see her mother on the ground, dead after some sort of lover's quarrel where Bonnie and her father had finally decided they could no longer deny their love.

And there was a dead body.

Only it wasn't her mother.

Coming around the bend, they entered a section of forest where the canopy of trees thinned, and the night sky shone brightly above. The lack of coverage gave the world a minuscule amount of light, but it was enough to illuminate the ghastly scene playing out in the graveyard.

Willa sucked in a sharp breath, and Noah halted abruptly as they assessed what was happening. In a heap on the ground lay her father, rolled to his side. Wearing his usual dull brown wool trousers and plain cream colored shirt, the blood from the wound on his chest soaked the material all along his front.

"He's dead, Dr. Anderson," Bonnie said, answering their unspoken question. "At least, he better be."

Scrunching her robe tightly around her, Margaret stood serenely beside her husband's body. She held a red lantern and, catching sight of Willa, clucked her tongue in disapproval. "Stupid girl. I purposely didn't give you the tonic so you could run off but look at you. Standing here, caught right in the thick of it."

"Now, now, Margaret. We'll not begrudge our Willa," Bonnie scolded. "Besides, it's working out for the best. Cal talks big but obviously can't handle things as promised."

The slice of a shovel greeting the earth finally registered through the buzzing in Willa's head. Consistent and strong, it carried like a metronome through the quiet, and she stepped to the side to see who was making the sound.

Beyond the black wrought iron fencing, beyond the high arch with its sharp spikes, mounds of disturbed dirt lay in piles throughout their family graveyard. Her brother's golden head would emerge from the earth every so often, synced in time to the sound of metal greeting the ground. Sweat covered his brow, and a second lantern hanging precariously from a post gave his features an eerie glow.

"Cal?"

A whisper in the wind tickled her ear with a reply. A song—a warning—there the whole time. *Go,* it said. *Run. Leave this place and never return.*

But she hadn't listened.

"Cal, come here and get this business over with," Margaret called out, nudging her dead husband's body with a booted foot. "I might not want this bastard buried in the same graveyard as our girls, but we don't have much of a choice."

Our girls.

Grace and Bonnie's baby.

Surprised that her mother knew Bonnie and her father's secret, Willa blurted out the first thing that entered her mind, "You knew about their baby?"

Margaret's brows shot up, her sharp eyes landing on Bonnie, who merely shrugged. "I brought her up yesterday during Willa's attack," Bonnie explained. "I wanted—*needed*—to see if he'd gained any remorse before we followed through with this, but no. He repeated the same story he's been spouting for the last twenty-seven years. He sat there and still pretended that my beautiful baby..." Her voice shook, the gun trembling in her hand. "That she didn't die by his hand."

The blood drained from Willa's face. Noah had snuck closer, and she clutched his arm to steady herself. "What?"

"And he would have killed Grace, too." Her mother approached, stepping over her husband's body as if he were nothing more than a dead animal in her way. "Had we not come in time, he would have murdered her just as he did poor Tommy."

"But he tried to save her!" Willa didn't understand why she was defending him, but she could recall clearly how distraught her father had been that day. "He mourned Grace."

Bonnie and her mother cackled together, their faces appearing grotesque in the moonlight. "He wasn't mourning Grace. He was mourning his freedom, thinking he might lose it if he were caught for killing Tommy," Bonnie said. "Stephen was selfish right down to his rotten core."

Noah calmly drew Willa away from her mother and Bonnie. "Why didn't you turn him in?" he asked. "If you wanted him gone, why kill him? Why not just turn him over to the authorities?"

Margaret ceased laughing, utterly appalled by his suggestion. "And endure a scandal?"

Bonnie shook her head. "No, that would never do. Certain scandals you can come back from, perhaps even pull a little sympathy due to the situation, but having Stephen outed as a murderer is not one of them."

A slow, calculating smile tipped the corners of her mouth. "So, we made plans. Yet, we couldn't move forward until the final piece of our puzzle was filled by you."

Frowning, Noah forced Willa behind him. "What do I have to do with this?"

"Well, in all honesty, we didn't know what to do with Wilhelmina," her mother answered coolly. "She's quite a lot of work, Dr. Anderson, and I hope you know that now that you've spoiled her for any other husband, we'll not be taking her back."

"We were going to let her go to Richards and hope for the best," Bonnie said. "But you are a much better alternative."

The blouse she had chosen to wear suddenly felt tight, and Willa choked on a sob. Noah spun around to cradle her face in his hands. "Look at me, Willa. We're going to be alright," he promised. "They're not going to hurt you."

A crazed look entered her mother's eyes, and Willa smartly quieted, having seen it before on the day Grace died. "This is what we mean. She's quite a bit of work." Marching to her husband, Margaret violently stomped on his face. "And it's all your fault," she screeched down at him. "You did this to her! You destroyed my daughter!"

Another strike, and then another. Over and over until Willa thought she might vomit every time her father's large body jarred from the impact.

"He said my baby couldn't breathe. I was nursing her, and Stephen asked if he could hold her when she was finished," Bonnie said, remaining composed through Margaret's crying. "Of course, I let him. He was her father. He would never hurt her."

Margaret ceased her battle with a dead man, huffing hard. Her hair had come loose from the nighttime curlers she often used, and she blew a strand from her face. "Tell them the rest. Tell them what he did."

"He said he wanted to take her outside and be the one to show her the world for the first time. I was so tired, you see, and couldn't go with them, so I took a nap while they were gone. When I woke, she was dead."

Bonnie's chin lifted, a single tear slipping down her cheek. "Six hours old, she was. My baby was six hours old."

"Did you see him do this?" Noah demanded. "Or are you just assuming that's what happened?"

"She didn't see him do it, but he confessed to it." Cal stumbled through the graveyard's archway and down the small incline to where they were all standing on the path. "Right around the time he confessed to what he had been doing to Willa."

"What he was doing to me?" Willa refused to hide behind Noah any longer, but he wouldn't permit her to move, holding her behind him in a vice grip. "What's Cal talking about?"

Cal stopped directly in front of Noah. "Do you love my sister?"

"Yes." There was no hesitation in Noah's voice. "And always will."

"Good." Bending down, Cal retrieved a shovel from the brush and held it out to Noah. "Then you can help me bury the sack of shit."

Noah didn't say no, only waited. "Explain to me what he did to Willa."

"You were such a beautiful baby, Wilhelmina." Her mother's lips pursed, and she crossed her arms, angling her head to look up at the swaying treetops. "Prettier even than Grace."

"My little girl looked so much like you." Bonnie came forward, lowering the gun finally. "And when you arrived, I fretted. I was worried that you would drop dead just as she did."

Cal held up a hand for them to stop speaking and addressed Willa. "Did you really believe Bonnie came to work at Haven House because she couldn't stand to be away from him even after he married our mother?"

"I-I...yes?" Willa didn't know how to respond. "Didn't you?"

"I did, at first, but when Grace died, I began to suspect that something was off," Cal replied. "Why would Bonnie stay with us all these years? Why were you the only one with an illness where there was no cure?"

"It's best to start at the beginning, Cal." Bonnie stared down at the man everyone had forever assumed she was devoted to. "When he married Margaret, I did still love him. That much is true. But when it became too much, and I tried to leave, he threatened me."

"Fairweathers own tiny plots of land in and around Hollingsdale," Cal said when Bonnie teared up again. "Nothing large enough to do anything with, but—"

"But my family's homestead sits on one of them," Bonnie interjected. "It's not a big place, a little clapboard house where I grew up."

Willa knew the house she was referring to. Bonnie would point it out when they went to town but never wanted to stop for a visit.

"He told her he would throw her family out of their home." Cal's already flushed and sweaty face twisted in revulsion. "He was going to do this to the woman he loved. A woman he manipulated for years, just so she would stay with him."

"And poor Bonnie began to understand how evil he truly was," Margaret added. "Lucky for me, I was never so disillusioned, but she was brave enough to question things."

"About my baby." Bonnie looked past Noah, aiming her words directly at Willa. "About how sick you were. I think you were eight when I first got an inkling that something wasn't quite right? Maybe nine? I listened to every quack doctor who came to Haven House, and none of them had a solution. It didn't make sense."

"You were always in the room whenever those doctors would come to Haven," Willa said, remembering how Bonnie and her mother would stand in the corner together, clutching hands as doctor after doctor examined her. "Neither of you ever left my side."

"He hired only idiots. None of those supposed doctors knew what they were doing, and when I confronted him during one of those horrible bouts where we almost lost you, Margaret and I urged him to get you to a real hospital." Bonnie replied wearily. "But he refused, saying that if it were God's will, you would get better on your own."

"And suddenly, your attacks lessened. We had our very own miracle right here at Haven House." Waving a hand erratically at the heavens, Margaret rounded on Noah. "Do you believe in miracles, Dr. Anderson?"

Noah shook his head solemnly. "I do not."

"Well, then, I guess you're both handsome and smart." Margaret's sneer returned. "There's no such thing as miracles, and if there were, a miracle would never grace the halls of Haven House. This place is cursed. This land is cursed. Stolen by the Fairweathers a hundred years ago, they doomed the entire line, damning it with an evil so eternal that it will take generations to purge from the blood."

"Enough!" Noah's shout bounced around the forest, sending the silently watching creatures scattering about in every direction. "Someone please explain what he was doing to Willa."

"I think you know, doctor." Margaret crept closer as if she were trying to examine something in Noah's expression. "I think the signs were there, but you're such a decent man that you couldn't accept what was in front of you the whole time."

"Tell me!" Willa demanded. Trembling in her fear and anger, she broke free of Noah's hold and came around to point a finger at the three of them. "Tell me now!"

Her mother and brother went quiet, allowing Bonnie to deliver the blow. "Poisoning you," Bonnie said without any hint of emotion in her voice. "Stephen was poisoning you and had been since you were in your toddling years."

Shock propelled Willa back, causing her to stumble over some vines winding through the edge of the path. "He was awful, but he wouldn't do that."

"Oh, yes, he would," Bonnie scoffed. "I followed you everywhere when you were little, seeing nothing but the ghost of my daughter growing before my eyes. It was then, when I tried to leave—when he threatened my family's home, and I remained steadfast in going—that you started having breathing attacks."

Willa shook her head violently, holding her hand up as if it could make Bonnie stop talking. "No."

"I couldn't leave you, girl." Bonnie approached a step or two but thought the better of it and remained where she was. "I didn't have proof of something going on, and neither Margaret nor I said a word, even to each other, but we both felt it. We both lived for years with this sick feeling. A feeling that screamed something about the whole situation wasn't right."

"But...but..." Willa couldn't believe it, and in her peripheral vision, she saw Noah making his way slowly over to her father's corpse, where he stopped to loom over it. "Noah?"

"The attacks would come and go, becoming worse as Wilhelmina got older," Margaret followed Noah, coming to stand on the opposite side of what was once her husband. "They always seemed to arrive around the time the mill's bank notes came due. Those pesky loans poor Stephen could never repay."

Noah's head snapped up, and Willa watched in horror as her mother burst into a fit of giggles. "Yes, Dr. Anderson. He used Wilhelmina's condition as an excuse for his inability to pay, and the banks ate it up every time, writing off the money owed as charity."

"How did he do it?" Noah's hands fisted at his side, looking ready to murder Stephen Fairweather all over again. "How did the bastard poison her?"

"On the far side of the mill, there are manchineel trees," Cal said, using his shovel's handle to point in the direction of the inlet. "They're deadly, and our *father* would take a drop or two of the fruit's juice and sneak it into Willa's food."

"Are you familiar with the little apple of death, Doctor?" Bonnie hedged up behind him as she spoke. "Every part of it is toxic, and when ingested, it can cause—"

"Swelling, blistering..." Noah's brows snapped together as he thought it all through. "I'm not sure what else." He glanced up at Cal. "And the only reason I know this is because *you* kept asking me about them when I came to visit Beau. I was intrigued and researched the plant."

"And what happens to the body when it swells and blisters repeatedly?" Bonnie pressed. "What happens when a little girl who is still growing gets some of that juice in her body over and over again? Not enough to kill, mind you, but enough to cause damage."

"Scarring." Noah turned to Willa, their gazes connecting. It grounded her, keeping her from floating off into some surreal unknown where none of this was true. "The throat is sensitive, and if repeated ingestion of the fruit's juice occurred, it would cause scarring and a narrowing of the esophagus. Enough so that any time there was a buildup of mucus, the condition would eventually progress into a type of acquired asthma. Or it would appear to be asthma."

Willa didn't think she could hear anymore. "Noah?"

He didn't respond, his gaze dropping to the ground while his mind worked through the madness. "I was told Willa choked on her food as a child. Is this correct?" He didn't wait for them to answer. "If she did, it was likely because of the fruit's poison. She could have aspirated on a piece and—"

"Our grandfather had a mistress, and when he ended things, the woman wouldn't let him go," Cal cut him off, impatient as ever. "According to what my father said, the old man poisoned her slowly with manchineel juice—just a drop or two every so often. He was hoping to make her sick, and it worked, causing the woman to have breathing problems."

"And your father took the information and applied it to Willa." Noah cursed under his breath. "Giving it so he could have a sick child and keep Bonnie close to watch over her, but then later drive the banks away when the money came due."

"Are you saying that I might one day not have this?" Willa hated the way she sounded so small and weak, but a tiny flare of hope had sprung in her heart. With Noah in her life, she had learned not to extinguish it at its first hint of warmth and anxiously waited for a reply. "Now that he's dead, are you saying that I might one day live without this fear that chases me every second of my life?"

The four faces staring back at her sobered all at once, with Noah's breaking her to the point of tears. "No, Willa. The damage is done," Noah told her. "In my examinations of you, I've found no evidence that would lead me to believe that your condition isn't a chronic one."

The dark forest spun in her vision, and the faint singing that had never truly left grew to a deafening level. In an instant, Noah was there, holding her in his arms so she wouldn't collapse. "But that doesn't mean I can't make life better. We'll go far from here and find a place to make our home."

"From what we can tell, he stopped giving her the drops of juice when the attacks would come on their own." Her mother lifted the lantern, her solemn stare filled with remorse. "At least, that's what Cal learned when he confessed."

Noah let go of Willa and charged Cal, grabbing handfuls of her brother's dirt-streaked shirt to slam him back up against a tree. "He confessed that he had hurt her, and you did nothing?"

"We devised a plan!" Cal struggled to get out of Noah's grip but was unable to. "The old man figured he was done for and that someone would eventually start asking questions about Grace and Tommy. That's when the drinking started. By the time last Christmas came around, it was at its worst, and he decided to sit me down to explain how to handle the mill should something happen to him. The longer we talked, the more he drank until he confessed his secret. He told me exactly how he kept the creditors away by using Willa's illness. I was shocked, of course, but listened. When he thought I was buying into his way of thinking, he told me about Bonnie's baby. Never let anything get in the way of your success, Cal. That's what he said."

Noah slammed Cal against the tree, and her brother's head hit with an awful smack. Before Willa could register what was happening, Bonnie had the gun aimed at the back of Noah's skull again.

"Calm down, Noah," Bonnie ordered as if scolding boys and not two grown men preparing to come to blows. "Margaret and I need Cal whole and well for this to work."

"He smothered his newborn daughter. He killed the man Grace loved and caused her death. He poisoned Willa," Cal snarled. "All in the name of his success."

"Success which amounted to a mill that won't be worth anything in five years' time," her mother said with disgust. "And a house in the forest, miles from civilization."

Willa's heart fluttered like the wings of a hummingbird. She had seen one once in their garden and marveled at the tiny creature, thinking it beautiful as it flitted from blossom to blossom.

But trapped in her chest, the painful ache of her accelerated heart caused a tightening not unsimilar to an attack, and she reminded herself to breathe through it.

"I love Haven House. I love the conservatory and the library. You made it beautiful. You expanded the place to where it doubled in size so I could have a world of my own," Willa said quietly, her strength depleting. "He might have made the place a living hell for all of us, but you made that house in the forest a wonderland."

Her mother turned away again, wiping at her eyes. "Yes, well, had I known we didn't have the money in the first place to remodel, you would still be living in the dilapidated manor I was brought to on my wedding day."

"What do you want with us?" Noah demanded, slamming Cal one last time against the tree before releasing him. "Willa needs to rest."

"Help us bury Stephen." Bonnie aimed the gun at Noah, who was stalking toward her as she spoke. "The holes have been dug, and everything is prepared, but Cal cannot move the body on his own."

Noah didn't hesitate and ripped off his coat. He came over to hand it to Willa. "I don't want blood on my clothes." He unbuttoned his shirt next, pulling it from his body for her to hold. The trousers came off finally, and he stood in the cold night air in nothing but his underpants. "Cal, you'll want to burn your clothes before sunrise."

"I can do that." Cal went to their father's head while Noah went to his feet. "We lift on three."

Willa watched as they hoisted her father in the air and made their way to the graveyard. She winced when they carried his massive body up the hill, and she was so focused on their progress that she didn't notice that her mother and Bonnie had moved to stand with her on the path.

"That is a fine man you have, Willa," Bonnie whispered. "A very fine man."

"I don't think we could have dreamed up anyone better for you," her mother agreed, positively riveted by Noah's partially naked form. "I hope you're prepared to pay attention and participate in the bedroom."

Bonnie chuckled heartily. "I don't think our Willa will have a problem participating with the likes of him, Margaret. She'll be pregnant before the spring. Mark my words."

"This is not the time or the place to be conversing of such things," Willa scolded, arching on her toes as the men reached the graveyard. It was hard to see past the wrought iron fencing, and she didn't want Noah out of her sight for even a moment. "And how do you plan to explain all of this to the staff? They must have heard you leave and the gunshots. Father's disappearance? How will you handle that?"

"I gave the staff a harmless sleeping tonic," Bonnie confessed with a shrug. "They'll wake in the morning completely unaware of what has taken place."

"And I gave the same tonic to Lucy when I came upstairs after you two retired for the night," her mother went on. "I brought her a tea. She sipped on it politely as I knew she would, and we discussed her wedding to Mr. Richards."

Lucy. The idea of abandoning her poor little sister had the hummingbird in her chest taking flight again. "You are going to allow her to marry Richards, aren't you?"

"I've given her my permission to marry next month." Her mother raised the lantern so they could see one another clearly. "Of course, only if we receive his promised dowry land in Hollingsdale."

"Our plan is to break down the mill and sell it in pieces for a hefty price," Bonnie explained. "We're hoping that Ulrich will purchase most of it now that the Andersons are loosely tied to the Fairweathers. If not, then one of the other dozen or so lumber mills across the area will be glad to buy its remains. Once that's complete, we'll use the funds to build a new grand home in Hollingsdale on Lucy's dowry land."

"Then we'll move on to Cal's idea of working with the empty land your father's hoarded for who knows how long," her mother said. "Tens of thousands of acres sitting empty for nothing. We control it all now that he's gone."

We.

"Cal will inherit." Willa could make out Noah and her brother's heads moving about in the moonlight but nothing else. "And you two control Cal, so you two control the Fairweather assets."

Her mother and Bonnie shared a look. "Your brother understands our plans clearly and will do whatever it takes to see them through."

"But you haven't told me how you're going to explain father's disappearance."

The two women grinned together again. "Cal has been practicing his handwriting," Bonnie said. "A note will be left."

"And the entire county already knows how Stephen loves to dally with serving girls." Her mother elbowed Bonnie with a conspiratorial wink. "We'll say he ran off with one of the Port Michaelson girls we kept on from The Gathering. A scandal, which, of course, we wanted to avoid, but this is the kind that we'll happily endure, as no one will miss him."

"Oh, think of it, Margaret. We'll have to beat the suitors away once we move to Hollingsdale," Bonnie said, sounding thrilled. "They'll be knocking down the door to get a taste of the poor abandoned Fairweather wife on their tongue."

"Let us hope so." Her mother continued to giggle in that obscene, high-pitched way of hers. "If Cal's plan doesn't work, we'll need some source of income, and I might as well have a little fun while I can."

The pair continued to discuss their future, and with each new step in their plan, Willa didn't know if this deranged conversation could get any worse, but when Margaret began practicing her false mourning face, she decided enough was enough.

"Excuse me." Bonnie's gun was back at her side, which Willa took to mean she was trusting them now that they had Noah doing their dirty work. "I want to check on Noah."

Leaving her mother and Bonnie to cackle over their vile plans, Willa hurried up the small hill to the graveyard. Her brother and Noah almost had the hole that was to be her father's final resting place filled.

Traversing the uneven ground, she reached them just as they finished, and standing over the freshly dug grave, a small part of her thought that perhaps she should feel something—anything—over her father's death.

But she didn't.

There wasn't an ounce of sorrow in her bones. Well, there was, but it was for herself. He had destroyed her body, destroyed the possibility of her living a full life, and for what? Money? Power? To be revered and feared by men who were as evil as him?

With sweat and dirt covering his skin, Noah tossed his shovel aside and held out a hand for Willa to return his clothes. "What else do you want from me?" he asked Cal.

"Nothing. Take Willa and go." Dropping his own shovel aside, Cal wiped the streams of sweat from his face and grabbed the lantern dangling from the fence. "I'm assuming I don't need to tell you to keep the events of tonight quiet."

With his pants on, Noah didn't bother with his shirt or jacket. "And I'm assuming I don't need to tell you to stay away from us." He crowded Cal, towering over him in his rage. "You will never contact us. You will never speak to my brother, my cousin, or anyone with the last name Anderson again."

Cal, being the stupid fool that he was, held his ground and raised the lantern in his hand, shining the light directly in Noah's face. "I plan to sell pieces of the mill to your family, but fine for the rest of it. I'll end my friendship with Paul and Beau, although they will find it odd."

"Then I suggest you use that calculating Fairweather way of yours to figure out how to make it not seem so odd," Noah replied in a low voice, looking ready to dig yet another grave and toss Cal in it. "You and I both know you're as manipulative as your old man."

Willa intervened as best she could, not wanting this to escalate and bring Bonnie back over here with her gun. "What of Jennie? Are you going to marry her, Cal?"

Her question made Noah grow angrier, and he whipped around, seizing her by the hand. "We're leaving."

Dragging her away from her brother, Willa struggled to keep up with Noah's long strides and ended up tripping on something protruding from the ground. "Oof."

Noah caught her by the upper arms before she fell, and Cal rushed up from behind to do the same, the lantern in her brother's hand dropping to the ground in his hurry to help. The candle behind the glass remained lit as it struck the soft dirt of the graveyard, revealing exactly what had caused her to trip.

A foot.

Thin and pale, the foot protruded from the disturbed earth, exposed as high as a few inches above the ankle where a piece of cloth could be seen.

No, not a cloth. A gown.

A nightgown.

With floral embroidery that Willa recognized immediately.

My mother made it for me right before she died.

A scream caught in Willa's throat, nearly bursting out of her if not silenced by Noah's hand covering her mouth.

"Hold it together until we get out of here, Willa," he whispered urgently in her ear. "They've all gone mad."

Cal kneeled, and setting his lantern upright, he lovingly stroked the foot with a single finger. "I'm sorry, Willa. I truly am. I'm sorry we didn't realize what he was doing to you sooner. I'm sorry for Grace. I loved her as much as you did and didn't mean to let their secret slip. I really didn't."

Calming slightly, Willa pressed herself against Noah's chest, and he released his hold on her mouth. "It was *you* who told Father about Grace and Tommy?"

Cal hung his head in shame. "I had no idea he would kill him."

Her heart broke for her brother. He must have carried the guilt of outing Grace all this time. "And you had no idea he would murder sweet Jennie, too."

"Why would he kill Jennie?" Her brother's golden head rolled up to face her, the lantern's light showing her a stranger laughing in ghoulish delight. "Oh, Willa. You're so naïve."

Noah dragged her away slowly as her brother rose to stand. "Father was right about doing whatever it takes to succeed. It's the only way to live, or else you become just another peg in the wheel, another body in the masses of mediocrity," Cal said, sneering at her ignorance. "We couldn't very well say he ran off with a serving girl only to have her deny the claim, could we?"

"No, no, no, no," Willa whispered, shaking her head as Noah continued to pull her with him down the hill. "No, Cal."

"Loose ends, Willa." Her brother's mouth twisted into a manic grin. "Always tie them up."

Hustling her now, Noah didn't speak when they reached the forest trail, and holding her hand, he hastened them past her mother and Bonnie.

"Never return, Wilhelmina," her mother intoned as they went by. "There's nothing for you at Haven House. Forget this place and let it rot into but a memory."

Firmly tucked at Noah's side, Willa buried her face in his chest, keeping up with his pace while she cried hysterically.

"Goodbye, little girl," Bonnie called after them as she and Noah neared the curve, so close to disappearing from their sight. "Willa only has a short life ahead of her, Dr. Anderson. Please make it a good one."

EPILOGUE

"The man at the general store said the place is haunted."

Striking a dip on the road, the Lincoln Continental bounced roughly, and Willa gripped Noah's leg to steady herself. Her bones were tired from traveling, and she knew his were too, no matter how much he tried to hide it.

"Oh, I'm sure it is haunted." Noah shifted in his seat and snuggled Willa closer. "But no more than any other old place."

Their granddaughter slowed the car's progress down the clay lane and peered up at the tunnel of oaks with its Spanish moss dangling overhead. "It certainly looks like it could be haunted," Anne mumbled, wrinkling her nose. "I know this is your family's land, but would you care to tell me why you want to see this place so badly, Nana?"

"I grew up here."

Willa smiled when their granddaughter spun around in the driver's seat with her mouth hanging open. "I knew you lived in Florida growing up, but I didn't know you lived in some old haunted house."

"It wasn't old when I lived here." Willa shifted in the backseat to peer out the car's side window. Just as she suspected, not much had changed. The overgrown forest hugged the road, obscuring her view of anything else. "Haven House was a grand home by the time I left."

"Haven House? You're telling me this place has a name? How very swanky, Nana." Anne turned back around and continued driving. "Pop, did you live near here too?"

"For a few months." Noah grinned at Anne's excitement. She was inquisitive to a fault, and he loved her dearly for it. "My family had a lumber mill about a mile from here, but their house wasn't as big as Haven."

"Oh, yeah. I remember." Anne leaned forward again, driving slowly as she took everything in. "That's the one that burned to the ground not long after you two got married, and since Uncle Beau was out of a job, it was how you convinced him to come up and run the practice."

"That reminds me that I need to phone Beau when we return to the motel tonight." Noah pulled a small memo pad from his pocket, jotting down the note. "Dr. Callahan has to check on Mrs. Johnson tomorrow, and Beau will need to follow up with him on his findings."

It had been a big step for Noah, but he had finally taken on another doctor at his practice. Even at eighty-eight, he didn't want to truly give up all his patients, but knew it was time to make that final transition into old age.

Willa hated that she was partially to blame for him feeling like he needed to remove himself from the day-to-day happenings at the practice. Her health had never been an easy thing, with her breathing issues at the forefront of their life. But to next have one's mind begin to fail was nothing short of adding insult to injury.

The gaps in her memory started a few years ago, with little things disappearing here and there. Now, it was hours or even days lost to her, and when it became noticeable, Noah finally decided to hang up his white coat for good, wanting to make the most of their remaining years.

What a wondrous thing it had been to spend a lifetime with the man she loved, to have children and grandchildren, and to have grand adventures with the small family she and Noah created. There were ups and downs, but always more good than bad, with neither minding as long as they were together.

After leaving Haven House that awful night, Willa never thought of the Fairweathers again. She didn't belong to them anymore, especially when she and Noah were married directly after the New Year. Their daughter Mary came along by the following autumn, and with a newborn to care for and another on the way shortly after, life became too hectic for her to give her old family a second thought.

"You'll need to call Robert tonight as well," Willa reminded him, proud of herself for remembering their son's schedule. "He's operating on a tough patient in the morning, and a few words of encouragement from you will help settle his nerves."

It turned out Ohio's climate worked well for her lungs, and Noah opened his family clinic not long after their son entered the world. Noah had dedicated his life to serving others but focused mainly on those with breathing difficulties so he could remain at the forefront of research on Willa's behalf. Their son had chosen the same profession and was as brilliant and caring as his father.

"Dad is always a bit looney before he hacks at people," Anne joked. "Mama likes to tease him and serve a big, rare steak dinner the night before."

Noah chuckled along with Willa. Their son's weak stomach was a long-running family joke.

Hitting the brakes hard, Anne let out a shout. "Goodness! Is that it?"

Through the trees, the white of Haven House peeked through. From her spot in the back, Willa couldn't see much but nodded. "That would be her, but who are those men at the end of the lane?"

Noah went on immediate alert, scanning the three large, surly men staring at them as if they were lost. "Don't drive any further, Anne. Let me go and speak with them."

"Pop, they're just workers," Anne assured him, pulling the car forward. "I wrote to Nana's family to let them know we were going to be in the area, and they said the place was being renovated. I thought I told you."

Willa shrunk in her seat. Anne had probably told her, but the information likely slipped off into the unknown corners of her mind. "I'm sorry, Noah. I guess I forgot."

Noah's blue eyes crinkled in their corners, and he squeezed her close. "It's alright."

Pulling the car forward, Anne parked directly in front of the house. Getting out, the three of them stared at the stark white columns, and Willa had to hold on tightly to Noah's hand when a jolt of nostalgia struck. "Oh, my."

Anne let out a whistle. "This is...Wow!"

"Can I help you folks?" One of the three men approached. "Haven House is private property, and the Fairweathers don't like people snooping around."

Straightening her spine, Willa looked down her nose at him. It was a Fairweather move she hadn't pulled in years. "My name is Wilhelmina Fairweather, and I am the sister of Calvin Fairweather."

"Oh, I'm sorry." The man stopped short. "I, uh, Mr. Malcolm didn't mention you would be stopping by."

Cal was dead. It was the only reason she and Noah felt as though they could come to Haven House one last time. They knew little of her brother's life, only that he married well and had three sons. The oldest was named Malcolm, and he had taken control of the family business, which they were calling Fairweather Holdings these days.

Willa didn't care for the name. She thought it sounded rather pretentious.

"What are you building out there, sir?" Willa asked, pointing at the bones of smaller structures out along the bayou.

The man smiled at her question. "With the war over, Mr. Malcolm wants to make this place into a retreat, and he's ordered us to construct cottages along the shoreline for extra guests who might stay over."

"Looks like you have your work cut out for you," Noah replied. "This old girl has sat vacant for a long time."

"Over fifty years, from what I hear. The forest and gardens were so overgrown when we started that they were nearly in the house." The man waved a clipboard at Haven. "Feel free to go inside. We've cleaned it up pretty well and plan to overhaul the interior soon."

Thanking him, they headed down the worn front walkway leading to Haven. As they went, Anne twirled about in the beams of sunlight peeking through the branches of the twin oaks standing guard. "Growing up here must have been a dream, Nana."

"Not really."

There was no need to elaborate. That part of her life didn't need to touch their precious Anne.

Pushing open the oak double doors, the three of them stood in the foyer, with Anne staring up at the gargantuan crystal chandelier. She pulled out her portable Kodak and took a photo. "Jeepers."

"It's a bit gauche if you ask me," Willa said, shuffling down the hall. She didn't want to stay long but was desperate to see her conservatory one last time. "I'm surprised my mother didn't take it with them when they moved to..." There went her mind again, damn it all. "Noah, what was the name of the house they built on Richards' land?"

"Something absurd." Noah took her arm, refusing to allow her to revisit the past without him. "Parkland Grounds, I believe."

Willa snorted. "Yes, that sounds like a name Mother would come up with."

Margaret Fairweather didn't get to live long enough to enjoy what Willa assumed was the grand home Calvin built for them. They received word that she died not but five years after their family abandoned Haven House and the mill.

On the other hand, Bonnie lived to a ripe old age and married a man from Tallahassee, where she spent the rest of her days in peace. She wrote to Willa only once, wishing her well and letting her know where life had led her.

Anne snapped another photo. "When I spoke to Malcolm's secretary, she said he couldn't meet with us because he was celebrating the birth of his son. I think she said they named him James."

She and Noah nodded, not at all concerned with the lives of the Fairweathers.

A cat darted out of the dining hall, startling them. "Bonnie's cats are still here!" Willa exclaimed, happy to see them. "If you find a kitten, grab one to keep, Anne."

Noah chuckled and kissed her temple. "What are you going to do with a kitten?"

"Cuddle it."

They entered the conservatory, and Willa stopped short. Nothing had changed. Not a single thing. Her piles of books and writings, the chaos of her mind—all of it remained as if they half expected her to return. A stack of letters caught her eye, and she recognized the handwriting immediately.

"Oh, Lucy."

John Richards had given her sister a happy life, even though their farm failed due to a sickness that spread among his animals. Through the letter from Bonnie, Willa learned Lucy and her family had moved somewhere further south, opening a grocery store that became quite successful.

Anne's camera clicked. "It's spectacular."

"This was my sanctuary," Willa told her. "I lived in this room every day."

"And I fell in love with her in this room." Noah nodded at the lower level. "Your grandmother was asleep on that sofa down there, and I sat and watched her for almost a good half hour, utterly captivated."

Willa rested her head on his shoulder. "Then he took me on a horse ride and had his dirty way with me on the beach."

Properly shocked, Anne gaped at them. "Don't tell me things like that."

"Well, then, I guess I shouldn't mention the little building a bit west of here." Willa wiggled her eyebrows at Anne. "We had quite a naughty time there."

"Nana!"

They toured the ground floor and spent the afternoon telling Anne the story of how they began. Willa had to sit every so often, not wanting to lose the momentum she was holding onto by a thread.

When they reached the library, she and Noah didn't bother to stop their granddaughter from stealing a copy of The Modern Prometheus.

Anne batted her eyes at them innocently. "It's not like they don't have two copies."

They decided it was time to go when the sun began to set.

"Thank you for allowing us to poke around," Anne told the foreman as they stood on the side porch. "Do you expect renovations will last very long?"

"Honestly, it'll take years," the foreman said. "She needs all new pipes and then the electrical…"

Taking the side porch stairs down the lawn, Willa ignored what the man was saying, too busy listening to the song coming in off the bayou. The locals were right to think Haven House was haunted. Her sister remained. Tommy, Jennie, and every other poor soul to lose their life on this land probably did, too. All of them, forever trapped.

Her mother had claimed there was a curse, and after so many years of being away, Willa believed it. She could only hope her father's soul had moved on. Enduring an eternity with him would be a hell unto itself.

"I wonder what the future will hold for this place," Noah mused as he joined her. "Whatever it is will have to be better than what she's already lived through."

Willa sighed, gazing out over the estate grounds and the bayou at its end. "My mother was right. This place is cursed," she replied, sending out a silent goodbye to Grace. "Haven House will never know peace. At least, not while the Fairweathers control her."

Ah, our *little apple of death* enters the scene again. Can you tell this plant traumatized me as a child?

While researching a certain character's untimely demise, I stumbled across two intriguing cases of acquired asthma brought on by the slow consumption of manchineel juice. Of course, I was appalled by the intentional poisoning, but also... with me being me... I just had to figure out how to use this awful information in my books.

And from there, Willa's story was born.

A writing exercise never meant to see the light of day, *If The Fates Allow* includes plotlines and characters long abandoned after the first Haven House drafts were completed. For example, Stephen Fairweather was our original Ben. Yes, that's right. Benjamin Fairweather, the man everyone loves, once had a much darker side. He was a ruthless manic in the early versions of *The Secrets That You Keep*, only calming when I finally agreed to give him Laura Jean.

Thank god for character development.

Speaking of character development, we see quite a bit in Willa. I hope you enjoyed your time with her, and I want you to know that you'll get to see her again in the series. Well, not Willa exactly, but her legacy. She and Noah went on to create a wonderful family, but even so, the Andersons still have that Fairweather blood running through their veins. Their addition to this universe is one that will be explored in the future, but I will say that the Anderson family's return to Haven House will come sooner rather than later.

As always, thank you for reading,
Chloe

FAIRWEATHER
FAMILY TREE

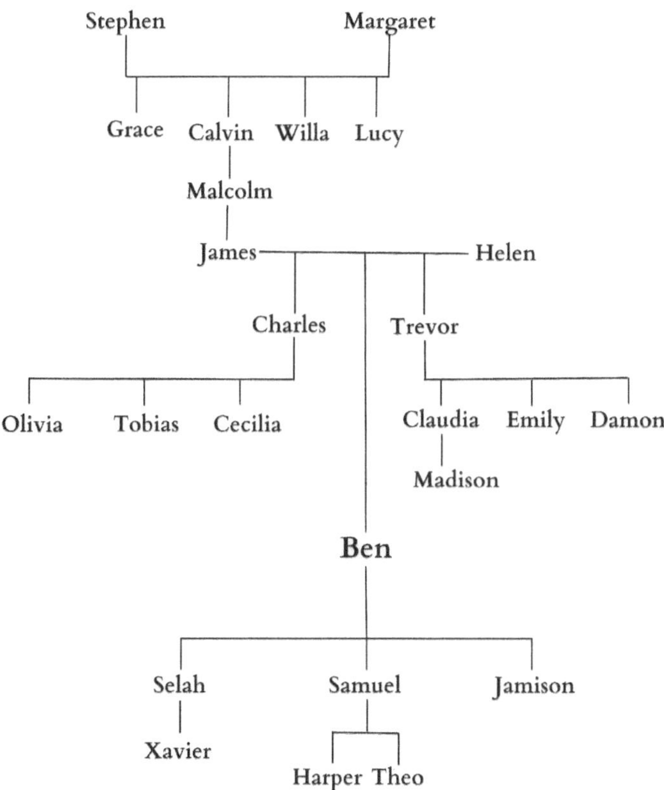

ACKNOWLEDGEMENTS

We all know I'm going to start by extending my thanks to Caitlin first. The poor woman is endlessly tortured by my constant off-the-wall shenanigans and ideas. You know what I mean. The whole thing where I say, "the readers won't care if I kill this character," and then Caitlin comes in to knock some sense into me. Spoiler: the very handsome Rowan McIntyre will live because of her, so say thank you.

Thank you to my husband and kids. If you didn't know this, my kids are the best humans in the world, and I could not be more proud of them.

Thank you to my alpha reader, the incredibly multi-talented Pamela Dawson. She has provided some of the best suggestions for this series, including the final gut punch in *Waiting For A Girl Like You.* So, when you're reading the last book and gasp at the end, that's Pam.

Thank you to my editor, Samantha Swart. She has been with me since the beginning of this crazy train. At least I kept the family small this time! That's progress, right? We have one more book to go before we close the doors of Haven House for good, and you and I both know it's going to be a wild ride.

Thank you to Jan Hurst, the world's best proofreader and sounding board. Twenty-plus years ago, she plucked me out of a crowd and said, "I'm going to mentor you." Like a good girl, I listened, and now here we are... getting technical with spicy scenes while she drools over an imaginary man. (Ben will always be yours)

My dear BETA Readers, thank you so very much! Kristina, Chasity, Mandi, Brandy & Kiah, all of you tackled this manuscript like pros and gave some stellar (and hilarious) feedback. As always, it was a pleasure, and I cannot wait to torture you more in the future.

Thank you to my Street Team! I told you I would include your names in one of these stories. This time, we see Jennie, Bonnie, and Grace hanging out at Haven House.

A huge thank you to author Nik Robbins for your undying support. I can't wait to see what the future holds for you.

My sincerest thanks to my ARC Team. You guys rock!

I would be remiss if I didn't mention the person to whom this book is dedicated. Dr. Merissa Hudson, I am so proud of you. You're the kind of badass most women aspire to be. Thank you for the years of friendship that began way back in the age of dinosaurs. I hope we will forever go trick-or-treating together and continue embarrassing our kids with our raucously loud laughter.

And many, many thanks to you, dear readers. Thank you for taking a chance on my books. I hope to bring you home to Haven House again very soon.

About the Author

Chloe I. Miller loves to write spooky, spicy stories that tend to make her readers cry. She lives on a beach with her husband, two children, and a dog that doesn't realize she's a dog. For more information on upcoming projects, you can visit www.chloeimiller.com.

Instagram: @author.chloe.i.miller
TikTok: @authorchloe.i.miller
Facebook: Haven House Reader Group

www.ingramcontent.com/pod-product-compliance
Lightning Source LLC
Chambersburg PA
CBHW021547310726
48972CB00003B/723